Hollywood
Spank

Shoshanna Evers

Hollywood Spank
Shoshanna Evers

When the studio heads for Mark Cannon's new action movie discover that their leading man likes to spank his personal assistants, they insist Mark hire a professional submissive who won't run to the tabloids with his kinky secret.

Andrea Landley may be a wonderful assistant, but she lied through her teeth about being a BDSM pro to get the job—and now her real career as an undercover tabloid reporter has gotten very interesting.

Andrea is willing to do whatever it takes to get the dirt for her scathing exposé—even if it means learning how to take a spanking from a movie star. She doesn't realize until it's too late that Mark Cannon has a lot more in store for her than just a simple stinging bottom.

Hollywood Spank © 2011 Shoshanna Evers
Original published by Ellora's Cave Publishing, April 2011
Edited by Jillian Bell
Cover art by Rob Sturtz www.SelfPubBookCovers.com

Print edition, copyright © 2013 Shoshanna Evers

ISBN-10: 0991372204
ISBN-13: 978-0-9913722-0-1

DEDICATION

For my husband, always and forever.

CONTENTS

ACKNOWLEDGMENTS

Thank you to my readers, first and foremost. Without you, I would be writing into the abyss. And a special shoutout goes to the Shoshanna Street Team—thank you for your support, and for spreading the word!

Hollywood Spank was originally published by Ellora's Cave Publishing in 2011. I'm grateful to them for letting me write all of the dirtiest fantasies that tickled my fancy, and for whipping my stories into shape. Thank you to Jillian Bell, who edited *Hollywood Spank*.

It's a thrill to be able to re-issue this short novel, three years later, as a self-published book, at a low price for my readers. I'm grateful for the many indie authors who paved the way, showing me a path that has allowed me to be a full-time writer.

Thank you to my cover artist, Rob Sturtz, from SelfPubBookCovers.com for my new cover! I co-founded SelfPubBookCovers.com with Rob to help fulfill my dream of having quality covers at an affordable price available to all indie authors, instantly. If you're a writer, too, you might want to check out the amazing artists we have on board!

Last on the list but first in my heart: thank you, Dear Husband, for being awesome. I love you!

CHAPTER ONE

Wanted—Extremely Discreet Personal Assistant.

The craigslist ad had been mysteriously brief, but Andrea Landley figured any job had to be better than the one she was going to be leaving. What on earth had the ad meant, saying that an extremely personal assistant was required and discretion paramount?

She would have skipped it entirely except for the fact that the interview was scheduled on the set for a new Mark Cannon movie called *Trapped in Action* shooting in the Los Angeles Valley. Her roommate Frannie was actually working on set already as a crew member. It wasn't every day Andrea got to go on a real live movie set, even if she did live in L.A.

If the interview was a bust, at least she'd get a chance to see the movie biz up close and personal—and maybe even get a glimpse of Mark Cannon, the sexiest leading man since...basically anyone ever.

The *Trapped in Action* set spread out around Andrea like a maze. Craning her neck to see the row of stars' trailers, Andrea nearly walked into the craft services table where snacks and beverages lay waiting for the cast and crew to nosh on between shots. She smiled with embarrassment and tried to maneuver herself gracefully past the electrical cords, ladders and huge lights that crowded her path.

The job interview had to be for an assistant to some bigwig. Someone who was too busy to leave the set and important enough to conduct job interviews in the middle of making a movie. Andrea walked carefully, keeping her eyes on a long line of women standing behind a folding table where a man in a suit was making everyone sign something. This had to be it.

"Is this the line for the job interview?" she asked a skinny girl with bleached blonde hair standing in the back of the line. The girl looked her up and down with a smirk and nodded. Suddenly Andrea's new jeans felt a size too small and she knew her long black hair had whipped itself into a mess as usual.

Andrea smiled broadly and then looked away. She was going to get this job no matter what it took. No matter what she had to sign. She couldn't stay a secretary for her on-again, off-again boyfriend and boss Rodney forever. She had a lot of potential, she just could feel it—but she'd been stupid to believe Rodney when he told her that working as his secretary at *The Hollywood Exposer* would someday lead to her working as a full-fledged reporter.

As the line got shorter, Andrea could see that once the women signed whatever it was they were signing, they went on another long line. Geez, it was like an amusement park. Just when you think you're done waiting you end up on another line to wait some more. Finally she got up to the guy in the suit.

"Sign here, initial here," he said.

"What am I signing?" she asked as she quickly scribbled her name.

"Basic nondisclosure agreement. The usual—you won't disclose who you see or what you do under penalty of law. Otherwise half of you ladies would run to *The Hollywood Exposer* or the *National Enquirer* or something with the story." The man in the suit took her agreement and filed it in a large portable filing bin set up on the grass next to him. "Résumé, please."

"Um, okay," Andrea said. But "secretary at *The Hollywood Exposer*" was on her résumé. "I actually don't have a résumé at this time."

The man nodded as if he wasn't surprised. "You're one of those. Fine, get in that line over there and face that trailer, please."

Face the trailer? Andrea stepped past the folding table and nearly fainted as a trailer door with a big yellow star and the name MARK CANNON came into view.

She was interviewing for a job as Mark Cannon's personal assistant? Wow. This was totally worth playing hooky from work.

An older woman in a pantsuit came forward and said, "Thank you all for coming today. Just a reminder, you've all signed an ironclad nondisclosure agreement. And I'm very litigious." She smiled, but it was obvious she wasn't kidding about suing the pants off anyone stupid enough to spread rumors. "Now I'm going to interview each of you privately, one at a time."

The line moved so quickly Andrea doubted she'd get more than a cursory glance before being dismissed. Watching closely, she could see most of the girls were quietly asked a question and then shook their heads no.

"Hurry up, you're next," the woman said briskly. "I don't suppose you have any experience in BDSM?"

"Of course I do," Andrea lied. The other girls had said no, so she'd say otherwise and get this job if it was the last thing she did. "Yes. Plenty."

Not that she had experience with whips and chains and dungeons and men walking their partners around by a leash and collar. She had seen the costumes some BDSM people wore in the Pride parade last year, though. It was probably going to be obvious by the fact that she wasn't holding a whip in her hand that she didn't really know much about BDSM, but she wanted this job. She didn't have a résumé she could hand in, so she'd just fudge the facts a bit and make up for in spunk and hard work what she lacked in actual experience.

The woman in the pantsuit nodded approvingly and sent her off to the side where only a few other women stood, separated from the girls who were sent home.

The woman in the pantsuit nodded to the first girl. "You—dominant or submissive?"

The girl smiled. "I perform weekly as a dominatrix at a private club. Mr. Cannon is welcome to come check out my show tomorrow night."

The woman in the pantsuit shook her head. "Pass." One of the other women in the small group shrugged and left as well. Okay, so they passed on the dominatrix. Good thing Andrea wasn't holding a whip after all.

Suddenly the woman was looking at Andrea and one other girl, the skinny bleached blonde who had smirked at her earlier. "So that makes you ladies our only experienced submissive applicants?"

Andrea smiled and nodded. Submissive...that was the person who wore the collar and got tortured. So maybe the movie they were making was about BDSM stuff and they wanted to make sure Mark Cannon had a knowledgeable assistant. If that was the case then she was in over her head already. She could fit the knowledge she had about BDSM into a thimble.

The bleached blonde pushed in front of Andrea. "I want to see him first."

The woman stepped out of her way as the girl practically barreled past her on her way up the trailer door steps to Mark Cannon's private dressing room.

Ten minutes later, the girl came out with her mascara running around her heavily made-up eyes. She turned to Andrea angrily. "You can have this stupid job. He's fucking crazy."

Andrea looked at the trailer steps and the big yellow star on the door and shrugged. She could do crazy. Rodney was kind of crazy, so she should be used to that by now.

Andrea's heart beat a mile a minute as she stepped up the flimsy stairs to Mark Cannon's trailer door. How could she introduce herself to one of the world's top leading action stars? He'd probably laugh in her face. It was times like this when Andrea wished she looked like—well, anyone else.

It could be pretty hard to live in Southern California, home of some of the most beautiful actresses and models in the world. Even the women who weren't in "The Biz" looked like they were, with their sculpted limbs and sun-bleached hair.

Andrea felt as though she always looked plain and boring next to them. Fortunately, she didn't work in front of a camera for a living. Her computer screen didn't care what she looked like. She'd raised her fist to knock on the door when it suddenly swung open.

There he was, in the flesh. The face that adorned teenage girls' locker doors and the body that gave women all over America naughty daydreams. Mark Cannon smiled at Andrea and his grin was white and perfect, just like it was on millions of movie screens and billboards everywhere.

Andrea willed her heartbeat to slow its frenetic pace. He was just a man, and she already knew what men were like. Besides, she had her unofficial-sometimes-boyfriend Rodney, even if he didn't like her that much. So she wasn't really available to date anyway.

Why couldn't she just stop thinking this way? It wasn't as if Mark Cannon would notice her even if she spontaneously combusted right here in front of him.

Then he smiled broadly at her and stuck out his hand. A lock of his brown hair fell over one of his sea-green eyes and Andrea had to restrain herself from brushing it away for him.

"I'm Mark," he said, his deep baritone voice reverberating through Andrea like a drummer whose sole purpose was to make her stand up and take notice.

He was even better-looking in person than on the silver screen. His hand enveloped hers and a jolt of excitement ran through her. It felt so big and strong wrapped around hers, she didn't want him to let go.

"That girl is not submissive," he said, nodding his handsome head toward the skinny girl that was already leaving the set. "And she sure can't take a spanking."

He pulled on Andrea's hand. "Well, come on then," he said.

Andrea stepped inside his trailer. Did he just say he *spanked* that girl? Was that what the nondisclosure agreement was about?

"I like how you don't speak unless you're spoken to," he said approvingly. "You must have experience."

Andrea just looked at him, dumbfounded.

"But I actually don't go in for all that formality. So…speak," he prompted.

"Y-yes sir."

"That's nice, calling me Sir. Maybe I'll go easy on you," he said.

"Thank you, Sir," she said immediately. "And I'm Andrea, by the way. Andrea Landley."

Why did he just say he didn't go in for all that formality if he wanted her to address him as "Sir"? Okay, she could totally do this. He was just another egomaniac, like her boss—her old boss. Because she was going to do anything, including taking a spanking, to get this job.

Suddenly it came to her. This was exactly the kind of thing Rodney would kill to hear about. This was the kind of thing legendary *Hollywood Exposer* exposés were written on. She could see the headline now, with her byline, of course. "Mark Cannon Spanked Me—The True Story of a Professional Submissive".

Now she just needed to get the gig.

"Nice name. Sorry about all the legal mumbo jumbo," he said, indicating the suits outside. "Once the studio heads figured out that I like to spank my assistants, they sort of stepped in and insisted it all be on the up-and-up. Have you done this kind of work before?" he asked, gesturing with his hand for her to sit on the little cot in the corner of the trailer.

Andrea sat carefully. "Yes Sir. Absolutely."

"For who?"

"I, uh, signed one of those nondisclosure agreements for him too. But I can get a reference for you. Sir." She smiled, hoping it was true. Surely Rodney would play along if it meant getting his hands on a story like this one?

Mark Cannon nodded. "It won't be all fun and games. I really do need a personal assistant. I have scripts that need highlighting, you'll need to run errands for me, pick up my mail and my coffee, keep tabs on my schedule, that sort of thing. Can you do that?"

This time Andrea didn't even have to lie. That job description sounded a lot like what she was already doing for Rodney. "Yes Sir, I can definitely do that."

"Then I just need to see if you can really take a spanking, or if you're going to run out of here crying like our friend there."

Andrea's pulse raced. She'd never been spanked before—not as an adult, not as a game.

"Drop your jeans, Andrea," Mark Cannon said. "And lean over the edge of the cot."

Andrea looked at the door for just a moment.

"I'm not here to fuck you, Andrea. I just have special needs for an assistant, as you can see. No sex. Just a spanking. Do you agree, or are we done here?"

Andrea smiled before resolutely dropping her pants and leaning over the cot. "Yes Sir."

The air caressed the back of her legs, and wished she'd worn sexier underwear. They were just cotton panties. She resisted the urge to look back at him over her shoulder.

Suddenly his palm smacked one of her ass cheeks through the cotton of her panties, then the other. It stung, but not enough for her to make any noise. Did he want her to make noise?

"May I drop your panties?" he asked.

"Yes Sir," she said. She felt his fingers linger along the edge of her underwear before he carefully lowered it, leaving her ass exposed. The next smack stung a bit more.

"Do you like that?" he asked.

"Yes Sir," she said immediately.

She realized she wasn't lying. This was weird, but it was fun. She'd never had a man interested in her like this before.

Smack! Smack! The spanking got harder and a little moan escaped her lips.

She gasped with pleasure as moisture pooled between her thighs from the spanking.

Oh my goodness. Did I just become a prostitute?

"Wonderful. You weren't lying when you said you like this," he said, pulling her panties back up and helping her pull her jeans up. "You're hired, if you accept the position." With a quick flick of his fingers, he zipped her fly.

This was a once-in-a-lifetime opportunity. She had to take it. "I would absolutely love to be your personal assistant, Mark Cannon."

"Um…just call me Mark. Or Sir. You don't have to call me by my full name."

"Of course. I'm a dork," she said before she could stop herself. "Sir."

"Not a dork," he said. "Beautiful. And I think this is going to work out nicely. Just step back out to that suit the studio made me hire and sign whatever it is he's got there."

* * * * *

She looks like a smart girl, Mark thought as Andrea raised her eyebrow at his remark. Smart and beautiful. Her creamy, pale skin had just a hint of a rosy blush in the apples of her cheeks, and was offset nicely by her long black locks.

Mark found himself wondering what it would feel like to run his hands through that hair and cocked his head to one side as he imagined the possibilities. He had told her no sex, but if she were willing…oh man, the things he could do to that luscious ass of hers.

He found he was suddenly intensely aware of her, this stranger walking out of his trailer door to go talk to the lawyer. She looked different from the women he usually dated. She looked…real. Mark kept watching her as she strode confidently up to the folding table and talked to the lawyer. Her breasts looked soft and so incredibly sexy that Mark knew they couldn't be fake. And to think that just moments before her arrival he had been wondering if everyone in L.A. had silicone instead of breasts.

Mark found himself daydreaming about what it would feel like to caress that perfectly natural body of hers. He wanted to tie her up, to play with her…how was he going to get any actual work done when he had such a perfectly lovely submissive assistant at his fingertips?

* * * * *

A flush of heat moved across Andrea's cheeks as she rushed out of the trailer and walked up to the man in the suit, who handed her a stack of papers an inch thick to initial and sign.

Mark Cannon had noticed her, and she didn't even have to catch on fire.

Andrea wondered how she had just scored the job, considering she looked nothing like all those other sexy girls who had come for a chance at the same position. Maybe those girls just hadn't figured on the position being bent over Mark's bed. He had gotten totally turned-on— and turned her on—just from spanking her. And here she was, not even able to arouse lust in her unofficial-sometimes-boyfriend and soon-to-be-former boss, Rodney.

Mark Cannon was known for his playboy ways. The tabloids had written stories on all of his "flavors of the week". Who knew that his taste ran to kink? She'd have to Google BDSM as soon as she could so she could learn the details of the sorts of things she had signed herself on for.

As for Rodney, well, he wasn't the romantic type—but a Saturday night date with her supervisor was better than another night alone on the couch with Peppers, cute as the tabby cat might be. Besides, they seemed to work well together, and that was about all she hoped for in a relationship with the opposite sex.

Being Mark Cannon's assistant was going to give her a front seat to all the behind-the-scenes action she could ever have dreamed of. If only he weren't so gorgeous. Andrea had to keep reminding herself not to stare at him. She couldn't believe she was actually going to be working for Mark Cannon. Frannie was going to flip out—she worshipped Mark Cannon.

Andrea scanned the contract quickly. Fully consensual, in good health, blah de blah, of age, blah blah blah, nondisclosure, etcetera. Rodney would help her get around the nondisclosure clause for sure, if he wanted the scoop for his tabloid. Andrea signed with a flourish and dropped the contract back on the lawyer's folding table.

"You can start immediately," the lawyer said. "Good luck. His assistants don't last long."

Andrea smiled. They just didn't have a good enough reason to stick around—like a huge story and byline in a national paper, even if it was a sleazy tabloid. Hell, maybe she could even write a book about it.

She walked back up the steps to Mark's trailer and knocked again.

"Paperwork out of the way?" Mark asked as he gestured her inside. Andrea nodded. "Wardrobe just dropped off my costume for this afternoon's scene, but in the future it might be quicker if I sent you to get it."

Andrea nodded vigorously. She had almost forgotten she'd actually have to run errands. She pulled out her notepad and pen to take notes.

Mark casually pulled his shirt up, revealing a taut, tan stomach rippling with his six-pack abs. Andrea covered her eyes with a gasp as he lifted his white T-shirt up over those famous broad shoulders and finally over his handsome head of hair.

"I'm sorry, Sir," Andrea said, peeking out between her fingers. "Did you need some privacy? Because I can step outside if you want…"

Mark's muscled torso kept filling her field of vision as she peered through her fingers. She could smell him…a warm, musky scent that was utterly masculine.

How could he just take his shirt off like that? Didn't he know what he was doing to her? She couldn't help but picture herself walking boldly up to him and running her hands across his smooth, hard chest. But that wasn't very submissive of her. She wondered what he would do— maybe he'd punish her?

Perhaps he would pull her close to him, crush her against his large frame and kiss her passionately until they were both panting and covered in a light dew of perspiration. Probably not. He'd said no sex, so no reason to fantasize.

Andrea spun herself around until the tempting vision of Mark Cannon was physically behind her.

Mark laughed. "Andrea, you drop your pants for me but you're afraid of a little skin? I'm not exactly the shy type. You can't be, in this business. And if you're gonna freak out every time I have to change clothes in my own dressing room, then this might not work out as well as I had hoped."

Andrea turned around to face him. She stared at the rock-hard muscles on his half-naked body openly, allowing her eyes to drink in his masculine presence.

"I'm sorry, Mark. I mean, Sir," she said quickly. "I guess I have seen you without your shirt on before…in that beach movie. What was it called? I'm sorry, I'm just not used to seeing men take their clothes off in front of me—"

Andrea clapped her hand over her mouth, mortified. She may as well just tell him she was a prude and get it over with, if she was going to keep saying stupid things like that. He was going to figure out that she wasn't actually experienced in being submissive or in BDSM if she didn't keep her mouth shut.

* * * * *

Mark smiled as he tried to stifle his growing laughter. Not used to men taking their clothes off, huh? He liked her sense of modesty. None of the hundreds of actresses or models that he'd dated seemed to think twice about getting naked. He could tell that for Andrea, seeing someone's unclothed body was still special.

Ever since Mark had gotten his first starring role in a feature film, it seemed he was able to get any girl he wanted—although it was a whole lot harder to get them *how* he wanted, which was over his knee. When he was between movies, he usually took a different woman out every night.

Mark tried to put a halt to the dating scene when he was actively in production on a film, though, because sexy young beauties often proved to be a bit too much of a distraction when he had to show up to the set for early morning calls.

He also happened to have a nasty habit of getting himself into trouble when his various girlfriends would find out about each other, usually just by picking up the latest copy of the tabloids.

Mark's smile nearly dropped off his face at the thought of those dreaded tabloids. Sometimes they got the facts right, but usually they seemed to distort the truth purposely just to sell papers. Sometimes they ran out-and-out lies about him on the front cover with two-inch-high headlines. The next week, they printed a tiny little sentence in the back of the mag, apologizing for getting their facts mixed up.

Mark knew it wasn't the tabloids' fault for his dates finding out about each other. After all, if he could just do what his mother was always telling him to do and find a nice girl to settle down with, the tabloids would have nothing bad to print. Marriage, however, just wasn't his style.

No woman could hold his interest for more than a few weeks, much less a lifetime. No one was exactly what he wanted in bed. He wanted a woman who loved being tied up, spanked, toyed with and whatever else he came up with. A woman who desired to be punished just for fun. The girls who threw themselves at him wherever he went were just there because he was a movie star. He never told any of them his true desires, for fear that once they saw what he was into, they'd run for the hills.

Mark wondered if anyone could ever love him for himself and not his fame or his money. How could they? The glitz and glamour of Hollywood blinded them. No one knew the real Mark Cannon, and if one of his dates did get to know him on a deeper level, he would fall off the pedestal she had put him on and her image of him would be smashed, along with any feelings she had for him.

"Mark?" Andrea's voice pulled him abruptly out of his reverie.

* * * * *

She picked up the shirt that the wardrobe department had sent over and gently fingered the soft, cottony material.

"So, Andrea," he said. "Are you gonna hold my duds for ransom or are you gonna let me get dressed?"

Mark was grinning at her, but as far as Andrea could tell he wasn't in any hurry to cover that perfect physique of his.

She smiled tentatively and handed over his shirt. She didn't know how she was supposed to act. How did personal assistants to the stars behave? Exactly what infractions would she be spanked for? Did he want her to make decisions on things, or could she expect to be told exactly what to do?

A flash of heat spread over her at the thought of Mark Cannon telling her, in his intense, deep voice, exactly what he wanted her to do. She would be only too happy to oblige...

Concentrate, you starstruck fool. Andrea forced the steamy thoughts from her imagination.

She didn't know a thing about this job. She would just have to play along until she figured it out.

Her heart skipped as Mark casually took his shirt from her. His strong, calloused hand brushed against her smooth pink one for one spine-tingling second and then withdrew abruptly, as if he, too, had felt the electricity that seemed to course between them.

Andrea tried not to look disappointed when he was fully dressed again. But that incredible body...oh boy. She had to stop this—she was acting as if she'd never seen a man before. And didn't Rodney count as a man? So what if Rodney didn't make her tingle. Tingling was for starstruck fans and schoolgirl crushes.

But what about that tingle she still felt on her ass cheeks? Did that count? Her panties were damp from her intense attraction to him. Just being near him, in his vicinity, had her lust spinning out of control.

Mark pulled his cell phone out of his jeans pocket and looked at her expectantly. Andrea stared at him blankly. Did she have something on her face or what?

Mark laughed and reached over to her, gingerly plucking her cell phone out of her tight jeans pocket.

"Oh," she said, laughing. "I'm an idiot. You need my number. Sir."

"Not an idiot, just refreshingly new to this," Mark said, smiling as he programmed his personal cell number into her phone and then called it, letting his own phone ring. "Now I gotcha," he said.

A loud knock pounded on the trailer door. "Mr. Cannon—we need you in Makeup in fifteen minutes," yelled a voice through the door.

"Thank you," Mark called back. He shrugged. "Guess I better head over to the Makeup trailer before I get in trouble for playing hooky." He gave Andrea a devilish wink. "You can hang out here until I need you. Just make sure to answer your cell phone when I call—I might need your, um, personal assistance for something." Mark flashed her one last smile before he had to duck his six-foot-two frame in order to step out the door.

Thank goodness. She couldn't think straight with him around. With Mark gone, she could focus. She pulled out her cell phone and quickly dialed Rodney's desk at the office.

"Rodney, it's me. You're never going to believe this." Andrea raked her fingers through her hair.

She could hear the clamor of journalists and who-knows-who else. Headquarters at *The Hollywood Exposer* was as busy as a three-ring circus.

"Andrea, babe, where the hell are you?" Rodney said, practically shouting to be heard. "I haven't had coffee all morning. The phone's been ringing off the hook and you wait until…what the hell time is it? Ten a.m.? Ten o'freaking clock to call me?"

Beads of perspiration gathered on Andrea's upper lip. "I'm sorry, Rodney. Ask Gloria to make the coffee and put anything you need typed into my 'in' basket. Maybe Stewart can answer phones for now, his desk is right near mine."

The line was silent. "Um…Rodney?" she said weakly.

"Damn it, Andrea. You're my secretary, not my boss, so stop telling me what to do. I tell *you* what to do. I need Gloria on our latest celebrity-turned-rehabber story. And Stewart stutters. Where the hell are you?"

Andrea took in a deep breath. "I'm inside Mark Cannon's trailer on the set of *Trapped in Action*."

That got his attention. She could practically hear Rodney salivating into the phone. "Are you serious?" he asked. "Where's my coffee, Gloria?" he shouted, not bothering to pull the phone from his face.

"Rodney, I'm serious. I just got myself a job as Mark Cannon's personal assistant for the duration of the shoot."

"How did you pull that off? We know you didn't charm him with your good looks," he snorted into the phone.

"Actually, I charmed him with my ability to take a spanking."

There was silence on the other end of the phone, which had probably never happened in the four years she had been working for Rodney. If that man knew how to do anything, it was talk.

Finally she heard him laugh. "Are you serious? *The* Mark Cannon likes to spank his assistants?"

"Rodney. I want to write. Let me write a story on my experience as Mark Cannon's submissive personal assistant—I swear I won't let you down."

"No way. You can spy on him and give the goods to me. I'll spin it into a scathing exposé."

Andrea lifted her chin in defiance, even though Rodney couldn't see it. "If I get the dirt, I get to write it. With my own byline. And…and a raise." Did she really just say that out loud?

"No raise. But this guy is a huge star, so…if you get all the dirt on him, I'll let you write the story."

"Rodney, thank you. You won't regret this. I'm not going to have sex with him or anything, I'm just going to let him do whatever it is people do with um, BDSM. I still have to do some research to find out exactly what that entails. I can get all the juicy details you'd ever want."

"I'm already regretting this…you're a horrible writer," Rodney said as he slurped his coffee loudly in her ear. At least she hoped it was coffee. You never knew with Rodney.

"Writing is my dream, Rodney. My life's dream."

"Then this is your big chance, girl," Rodney said and hung up on her.

Her article, published. Finally, after years of working as a secretary, she was on her way to realizing her dream. She could be a real journalist.

Andrea couldn't wait to begin her new cover job as a personal assistant. She just wished she weren't walking into this job with ulterior motives. Rodney, of course, was counting on the fact that Mark Cannon's taste for kink would provide tons of fodder for her article. Mark had dirty secrets just waiting to be discovered by a brand-spanking-new, hard-working undercover reporter such as herself.

Andrea looked around the inside of Mark's trailer. Pretending to be his assistant put her right in the thick of the action and gave her all the inside scoop she could ever have dreamed of—but could she be as brutal in her exposé as she had to be? She *did* want to show the world what she could do. She'd been on the sidelines for too long—so no man was going to keep her from her dream of being a journalist. Certainly not a man like Mark Cannon—a hot movie star who always got what he wanted.

In her desk drawer at home, Andrea had a pile of unpublished articles and stories that she'd written but could never get up the nerve to send out. When she had gotten the courage to show Rodney her work, he told her not to quit her day job as his secretary. But now...this was the first time Rodney ever agreed to give her a real writing assignment. She couldn't blow it.

She didn't know how much time she had alone before Mark came back to his trailer. She'd have to borrow his laptop and do some research.

She popped open the top of the laptop and frowned when she saw it was password protected. Tentatively, she typed in her best guess at a password based on her brief encounter with Mark.

S-P-A-N-K. Wow, that was easy. Instant access. She

must have missed her calling as a hacker.

A few clicks later and she had more information about bondage/domination and sadomasochism than she knew what to do with. Some of it seemed kind of extreme and a little scary, and some of it seemed right up her alley. If she just didn't ask stupid questions and showed that she really was eager to please him, it shouldn't be too hard to fit in to the scene, right? Was being a dominant movie star's extremely personal assistant really the scene, anyway? What exactly was "the scene"?

She sat with an audible sigh on the little cot in the corner of the trailer. This was where Mark Cannon himself must lie down…the thought made her stomach do a somersault. She leaned over and sniffed the pillow, feeling like a weirdo even as she was doing it. It smelled like cologne. Mark's cologne. *Don't just sit here sniffing Mark's stuff like a psycho*, she warned herself. Who knew how soon Mark would call for her, or worse, walk in unannounced?

A white envelope that lay on the edge of the cot caught her attention. It was postmarked from New York. Maybe it was a fan letter, or a letter from his mom or something. Damn, the envelope was still sealed.

Andrea looked longingly at it as her newfound undercover reporter's instinct for dirt took over, but she couldn't give in to temptation and open it. If she did, Mark would know that she snooped and she could kiss her opportunity to write her exposé goodbye, along with the chance to learn more about this BDSM stuff from him. The mysterious envelope would have to wait.

"And that's the only thing in here worth snooping for," she mused quietly, smoothing her hand over the plain blanket that covered the cot.

She lay down, for no other reason than that she wanted to lie where Mark had.

She knew it would be a bad move to be caught in bed on her first day on the job, but it had been almost forty-five minutes since Mark had left to go into Makeup.

Andrea reasoned that they had probably whisked him off to get some scenes filmed—or as her show-biz roomie would say—"a shot or two in the can" before they had to break for lunch.

The cot sagged in the middle. Andrea got chills just realizing that his body had probably pressed against the cot in the same place she was lying now. Why was she thinking like this—with this awareness?

She had never felt this primitive, animal lust for any man before. She certainly had never felt anything like that for Rodney. If anything, Rodney inspired tepid boredom, not the hot, lightning-strike passion that Mark had mysteriously created in her.

She wanted to feel the weight of Mark Cannon's body as he lay on top of her. Those big, strong hands of his stroking her flesh as her arms were tied up above her head, like in those pictures she had just seen online…

Andrea closed her eyes as she daydreamed, images of Mark Cannon's startling green eyes coming to her unbidden.

Andrea thought she was still fantasizing when the door to the trailer creaked open and Mark stepped inside.

Her eyes flew open—but she was frozen on the cot, too startled to move as Mark stared at her lying there.

CHAPTER TWO

Mark stepped quietly into his trailer and placed his script on the little desk. The sight of the slender, beautiful young woman lying on his cot caught him off guard and he swallowed a gasp of surprise. His new personal assistant.

Despite how busy they'd had him in the last couple of hours, Mark had been unable to get Andrea off his mind. He had almost flubbed a line, since his thoughts kept wandering back to his trailer and that amazing ass of hers.

And now, to find her sprawled out on his cot, looking so sweet and...inviting, he could see why she had proved to be so distracting.

His gaze lingered over her long, shapely legs, clad in tight denim jeans, then traveled up her fitted long-sleeve blouse, its deep V-neck revealing just a hint of the swell of her perfect breasts.

He could stare at Andrea like this for hours and never get bored. Mark wanted to pull those tight jeans off her gorgeous legs and ravish her right then and there. His cock thickened at the very thought of having sex with Andrea. Too bad he promised her he wasn't there to fuck her...and too bad she agreed there would be no fucking.

Andrea crossed her arms over her chest and looked up at him.

"Uncross your arms," he said. "I want to see your breasts."

Andrea slowly uncrossed her arms and actually blushed as she did so, even though she was fully dressed.

"You aren't really experienced as a submissive, are you." It was a statement, not a question. She had lied. It was obvious now that this was all very new to her.

Andrea gasped and shook her head. "I'm sorry, Sir. I just really, really wanted this job."

"Enough to let me actually spank you?" he asked, surprised.

"I may have lied about my BDSM experience to get the job, Sir, but I wasn't lying about my skill as an assistant, and you saw for yourself that…what you did turned me on."

Mark looked at her thoughtfully. "That's true. So let me get this straight. You're a very good assistant and you're fully willing to explore the idea of me spanking you."

"Yes."

"Because it turns you on."

Andrea blushed again. Man, that was cute.

"Yes," she said softly.

"So even though I said no sex before, if all this really turns you on, are you willing to get a little sexual?" He sat on the edge of the cot next to her and held her chin in his hand, forcing her to meet his eyes.

"I just met you, Sir, and I don't usually have sex with men I just met," she said. "I mean, I never do. So, can we get a little sexual without actually having sex, for right now?"

Mark grinned. "Absolutely."

"So I can stay?"

"Say, 'Sir, may I stay?'" Mark said.

Andrea didn't hesitate. "Sir, may I stay?"

"Yeah, you can stay. But I want you over my knee right

now for lying to me."

"Thank you, Sir. For the job, I mean," Andrea said as she nervously draped herself over his lap.

He locked his legs around hers to keep her from escaping her punishment and raised his hand, relishing that moment right before he brought it down on her ass. "Say thank you for the spanking too."

"Thank you, Sir."

"My pleasure," Mark said. "And hopefully, it will be your pleasure as well."

* * * * *

When Andrea got home that evening, there was a note on the fridge from Frannie.

Did you get the job? I'll be at LouLou's with some of the crew from the movie if you want to meet me.

—Frannie

Andrea opened a can of cat food for Peppers, slicked on some lip gloss and headed back out the door. One of the best things about living in L.A. was the nightlife. Any night of the week, late or early, there was something cool going on.

Up-and-coming bands played in bars for a reasonable cover charge, dance clubs kept music pounding until sunrise and comedy clubs had open-mic performances that showcased anyone brave enough to get up in front of an audience.

LouLou's was a dive bar that was just beginning to become trendy thanks to its proximity to Universal Studios. Andrea walked through the front doors and looked around.

"Andrea, over here." Frannie's high-pitched voice rang out over the background music. Andrea looked around until she spotted her friend's mop of curly hair.

"Frannie," Andrea sighed with relief and walked over to her. She was sitting at a booth with two young-looking guys.

Frannie pointed to a man with a goatee. "This is

Donnie," she introduced him, "and this," she said, pointing to a man with glasses and a flirtatious smile, "is Steve. They're also working on *Trapped in Action*."

Andrea smiled at them. "I'm Andrea." She looked at Frannie out of the corner of her eye and paused for dramatic effect, barely able to contain her grin from leaping off her face. "And I'm working as Mark Cannon's personal assistant." She flashed the photo ID the studio security had hooked her up with.

Frannie screamed at the top of her lungs and nearly leaped over the table to throw her arms around Andrea. "Oh my gosh...that Craigslist ad was for Mark Cannon? No wonder it said discretion was required."

Andrea blushed. That definitely was not the only reason the ad said that. She motioned to Frannie to talk with her away from the other crew members. "Rodney's pretty excited about it too," Andrea said, glancing back at Donnie and Steve. "He thinks it could make my career at *The Hollywood Exposer*. I've been upgraded from secretary to actual reporter."

Frannie's smile lit up her face. "It's about time that jerk stood up and took notice of what a great writer you are. So now what? You get to interview Mark Cannon, right?"

Andrea avoided her best friend's gaze. "I suppose I could," she said slowly, "but I'll be taking a more, well...secretive approach."

Frannie's expression showed that she knew what Andrea was getting at. "He's my favorite movie star, Andrea," she said quietly. "I know you must be excited about this opportunity, but...you're not going to write something horrible about him, are you?"

Andrea felt a rush of guilt as she looked at her friend's face. "Not horrible, exactly. But I kind of have to write what sells, Frannie."

"But it's Mark Cannon. Do it to anyone else, not him," Frannie pleaded.

"You don't even know him, Frannie. You just think

you know him because you've seen all his movies."

"Oh, and you're the expert on Mark Cannon now?" Frannie said. "You've spent one day with him."

"Frannie, I don't want to fight. I promise you this—I won't print a single word if I can't prove that it's one hundred percent true."

"Look," Frannie said. "I know you—and I know you're a good person with honest intentions. It just sucks that your loyalties lay with a tabloid and that creep Rodney instead of with *the* Mark Cannon."

"This is the chance I've been waiting for my whole life. This is big. Really, really big. Can't you see that?"

"I thought the chance you've been waiting for your whole life was to write for *The Los Angeles Times*," Frannie reminded her.

Andrea rolled her eyes. "If there's one thing I am, it's realistic. Writing for *The Exposer* is as good as it's gonna get for me, and I have to give it my all or I'll never forgive myself."

"If you ruin Mark Cannon's career, I'll never forgive you, either," Frannie said. "Because in case you haven't noticed, now that I'm working on his movie, Mark Cannon's career is directly linked to mine. And if you screw him over and they find out we're roomies, I'm the one who will get fired."

* * * * *

The shrill ring of her cell phone woke Andrea before dawn.

She looked at the glowing red numbers on her alarm clock in confusion. Who was calling at this hour? She blinked until the numbers came into focus. Four a.m. Mark had told her his call time wasn't until seven.

"Hello?" she murmured into her phone.

"Rise and shine, sweetheart." It was Mark Cannon's strong baritone, unmistakably.

"It's four. In the morning." Then, realizing that this was supposed to be her job, she forced herself to sound more awake. "And I am wide awake and at your service. What can I do for you, Mark? Sir?"

"Venti sugar-free double-caf skim mocha latte. And if you could pick up my mail from my post office box, too, that'd be great," Mark answered.

"No problem, Sir. Coffee and mail."

"Meet me at my house in an hour." Mark hung up before Andrea had time to protest. He had given her directions yesterday.

She dressed quickly, throwing a purple sweater over her shirt to ward off the early morning chill. Her still-sleepy eyes looked back at her as she glanced at herself in the bathroom mirror. *Wake up*, she thought, washing her face vigorously. She toyed with the idea of skipping makeup completely, but settled on applying just a little mascara and lip gloss.

"Be good, kitty o'mine," she said as she opened a can of cat food for Peppers and rushed out the door. "Guard the house for Mommy."

At the twenty-four-hour mail center, Andrea punched in the code for the combination lock and pushed open the door, searching for Box 291. Mark had given her the code and the mailbox key yesterday, surprising her with his show of trust.

"My, my, aren't we popular today?" she said under her breath. The box was packed with fan letters. Some were hand-decorated to make them stand out.

Good grief. She would need a bag just to carry all of the envelopes. Why didn't she ever think ahead? She looked around the deserted room, the metal doors to the individual mailboxes stacked one on top of the other along the walls.

Not finding anything to hold Mark's mail in, Andrea stripped off her purple sweater and stuffed the fan mail into it, tying the long sleeves together. She smiled to herself as she viewed her makeshift mailbag. She hoped the thin, sleeveless blouse she had on under the sweater would suffice in the chilly morning air.

Of course, the wind nipped at her bare arms as soon as she stepped outside. Next time she'd really have to plan better.

A quick stop at Starbucks for Mark's venti sugar-free double-caf skim mocha latte and she was on her way to the multimillion-dollar gated community that Mark Cannon called home.

* * * * *

"Welcome to my humble abode," Mark greeted her at the door to his huge, modern house. Glass windows ran from floor to ceiling, making the view of the predawn sky part of the front hall.

Andrea tried not to let her jaw drop. This place was amazing…and not exactly a humble abode by any stretch of the imagination.

"I didn't realize I'd be so welcomed at this hour," Andrea said with a smile, handing Mark the two steaming Starbucks cups so she could set down her stuff. She wondered if he knew how good he looked with his hair all mussed up like that.

"Of course you're welcomed, you bring caffeine," Mark said. "Oh good—you're wearing sneakers. I forgot to tell you I do a hike with Sally every morning."

Sally, Mark's shaggy labrador retriever, heard her name and came bounding into the front hall.

"Sally, no!" Mark yelled sternly as Sally jumped with both paws on Andrea's slim shoulders.

Andrea shrieked and took a step back, tripping over the sweater full of letters she had set down by her feet.

Within seconds, Andrea was on her back, the exuberant yellow lab licking her face.

"Sally, get off of her." Mark pulled Sally up and looked over at Andrea. "I'm so sorry. I love seeing you on your back, but not like that," he joked.

"I'm fine, Sir, I'm fine," Andrea said, brushing the yellow strands of dog hair off her jeans, her legs splayed in front of her on the marble floor.

"On the bright side, she likes you."

"Lucky me," Andrea laughed. That dog really was quite adorable, in a slobbering kind of way.

"Actually," Mark said, holding out his hand to her, "she doesn't do that to everyone. She must think you're special."

Andrea reached her hand to his and let him lift her gently from the ground. His biceps flexed through his T-shirt as he pulled her up.

She nearly stumbled into him, then steadied herself, laughing to cover her embarrassment.

Mark shook the envelopes out of her sweater and handed it to her. "It's cold outside, you'll need this. You can grab the mail when we get back and answer it for me later."

"You want me to answer your fan mail?" Andrea asked in surprise as she pulled on the sweater. She followed Mark and the dog into the large kitchen to drop the letters on the table. "I mean, yes Sir."

"Sure. I trust you."

Andrea smiled at the thought of her, a tabloid reporter, being given permission to go through Mark Cannon's mail. She remembered that one mysterious envelope in his trailer. Why did he have it separate from his fan mail?

Suddenly it hit her. That letter was addressed to Mark's house, not his well-known P.O. Box. Whoever had sent that letter knew him, and knew him well.

Today would be a good day to find out just what was in Mark Cannon's personal mail. She could see the headlines now…

"Before we go," Mark said, "I want to help make the hike a little more interesting for you."

Andrea looked at him blankly. Interesting?

"Come upstairs for a minute," he said.

Andrea followed him up the long winding staircase, her pulse racing as she wondered what he was thinking. She had already agreed that she was willing to get a little sexual with him as long as no actual sex was involved—was he going to take her up on her offer?

"In here." Mark opened his bedroom door and gestured her inside.

Andrea stepped past the doorway and just stood there, unsure of herself, as Mark walked over to his dresser and pulled a package out of the bottom drawer. It was some sort of toy, still wrapped in plastic. Andrea stared in confusion.

Mark laughed. "I know you're new at this, but have you really never seen a butt plug before?"

Andrea shook her head mutely, suddenly terrified. That sounded suspiciously as though it was supposed to go in her asshole.

"Don't be so afraid. I'm not going to initiate you into anal play right this second."

Andrea breathed a sigh of relief.

Mark gestured toward the bed and she sat down heavily. "This," he said, "is going in your pussy."

She nearly fainted. "Oh," she squeaked.

"Don't move a muscle. Let me do all the work," he said. Andrea didn't think she could move even if she wanted to, she was so nervous, although she had to admit she was intrigued.

Lying back against the plush pillows that covered the head of the bed, Andrea watched Mark as he carefully unbuttoned her jeans and tugged them off her legs. She hoped he wouldn't notice them trembling. He slid her cotton panties off, letting them dangle from her ankle.

"May I?" he asked.

She had no idea what he was asking permission for, but she nodded anyway. He reached out and gently stroked her clit with one long finger. She moaned, it felt so good. Too good. She wouldn't be able to concentrate if he kept that up. He picked up the pace, alternating fast and slow, gentle and hard, until she was practically begging for release. But before she could come she suddenly felt the huge plug at the opening of her pussy and with one swift, hard thrust, it was inside her, nudging against her G-spot.

Mark wiggled the base of the plug, causing it to rock deep inside her, rhythmically hitting her G-spot again and again. But he still wouldn't let her come. He pulled her panties and jeans back up over the plug in her pussy.

"Get up," he ordered. "We're going on a hike, and you're keeping that inside your tight little cunt."

* * * * *

Mark glanced back at his assistant, her breath coming hard and fast as they climbed the upward slope of the dirt-packed trail in the Hollywood Hills. Was it the exercise or the plug pressing her G-spot that had her all worked up? He'd have to tie a crotch rope on her next time and get some clitoral stimulation going at the same time. Tomorrow, maybe.

Sally had raced ahead of them, her tail wagging and her tongue lolling outside her mouth as she enjoyed her morning run.

Andrea's dark hair whipped around her face as she hiked, her sneakers pounding the ground.

She was so beautiful...he couldn't stop looking at her. Her sweater clung to her body in all the right places, emphasizing her soft curves and flat stomach.

"So," Mark said, his breath slightly ragged from the climb. "I bet you didn't count on getting a workout when you took on this job, huh?" He laughed, his leg muscles burning with exertion.

Andrea smiled at him, her white teeth flashing in the predawn haze. They were slightly crooked, a refreshing change from the L.A. norm. "I love it, Sir. I'm going to need a daily workout if I keep eating off of that craft services table."

Mark shook his head in disbelief. "Are you kidding? With that body?" He let his eyes linger over her slender hips, but when he raised his gaze to her eyes he became aware of the deep blush blossoming on her face.

Andrea cleared her throat.

Mark dropped his gaze abruptly to her lips. A fine dew of perspiration covered her upper lip.

"I love set food," he said. "I used to be so broke when I was first starting out that the only decent food I'd eat all day was the free food on the set. Well, that and the meals I scored waiting tables."

"No way," Andrea said, rolling her eyes. "I mean, if you say so, Sir."

"Seriously—when I was new to the game, I used to work a day job as a waiter. If I got a couple of lines on a show or something, I had to skip work without pay."

"Somehow I can't imagine you as a waiter," she said. "When was the last time you even got your own coffee?"

"It's been a while," he conceded. "And I'm going to let that tone slide for now since you're being such a good girl. But I paid my dues, you know? Once you factored in the cost of transportation to and from the shoot," Mark continued, his feet pounding up the path in time to his words, "plus the cost of dry cleaning my own clothes that I wore on the set, and my headshots…"

"I bet you ate a lot of those instant noodles."

"Yup. Wouldn't change it for the world, though. I think it really made me appreciate what I have now…" He looked away from her. "Fame and fortune isn't everything, though. I'm still looking for something."

"Something?"

"Something's missing," he murmured, so softly Andrea didn't think his words were even meant for her. "Hey, Sally, wait up." Mark took off after his dog, who had doubled her speed and was now way ahead of them.

Andrea glanced at his perfectly shaped backside as he ran after the yellow lab. The fitted pants covering the lower half of his body were expensive designer jeans that were somehow casual, intensely rugged and masculine all at once. She licked her lips.

Perhaps it was Mark himself who was casual, rugged and masculine. And admiring his clothing was her subconscious way of noticing it, she mused. That man would look good in a torn sheet. Hmm, *especially* in a torn sheet.

The plug inside her made her feel so…filled. She had already had two orgasms while walking that she was too embarrassed to say anything about. They were deep, melting orgasms from the plug stimulating her G-spot as she moved, something she'd never experienced before. It definitely made the exercise, which she usually shunned like the devil, a lot more enjoyable…

"Wait for me." Andrea quickened her pace. "You know, I thought you had this, like…privileged upbringing," she said, out of breath.

Mark had caught up with Sally and was resting on the path, his big hand casually stroking the dog behind her ears. The sun was just beginning to rise and the cold was gradually dissipating from the air.

Andrea thought she saw a blush creeping up Mark's face, but perhaps it was just the early morning sunlight highlighting his features and giving them an irresistible pink glow.

"No," Mark said. "That was just publicity stuff."

"What? The years in India? The boarding schools and ski trips and the best drama coaches that money could buy?" Andrea asked incredulously. "Your bio says you were discovered by a studio executive, riding your horse at an equestrian show, and he got you an audition for that western movie. Sir."

"Publicity. I've never been to India, and my riding skills would never win me any equestrian trophies. I was unknown and completely broke until about five years ago."

"But your bio said—"

"So I take it you've checked out my website?"

Andrea arched her eyebrows. "Yes Sir."

She couldn't believe she had just admitted that she had

Googled him. Now he'd think she was just some smitten fan. She was looking for anything about his kinky side, but amazingly there was nothing to be found. Maybe those ironclad nondisclosure agreements really were, well...ironclad?

Mark started back down the path, whistling for Sally.

"You can't believe everything you read. It's just a bio for press releases," he said, bounding down the trail.

"But the whole thing was made up?"

Mark stopped abruptly and stared into Andrea's eyes. "Look, Andrea, people expect me to be a certain way. There's this glamour that got stuck to me when I got shot into the limelight. There's nothing special or glamorous about being a skinny little runt as a kid, without a penny to my name. Bullies were always beating me up on the playground. I lived in a crappy apartment that smelled like cigarette smoke."

Andrea stared at him, trying to visualize Mark Cannon the child.

"So now that you know, do I still seem like the perfect movie star? Could I still be your knight in shining armor, now that you have that pathetic visual of my real life?"

"It's not pathetic, Sir." She stood in front of him, looking up into his green eyes.

"But could I still be your knight in shining armor?" He reached out and cupped her face.

Andrea took a deep breath and exhaled. His hand on her cheek felt so...right. He leaned down and pressed his lips against hers and suddenly they were kissing. A light breeze blew across the back of her neck and she was faintly aware of the beautiful hills surrounding them...but all of that faded into the distance compared to the experience of kissing Mark Cannon. Just this morning he was rubbing her clit, but somehow this simple kiss felt so much more intimate.

Mark pulled away and looked at her. "I'm sorry. I don't know what I was thinking. I wasn't planning on kissing you like that."

"It's okay, Sir," Andrea said, even as the thought flitted through her mind that Rodney would probably be pissed off if he knew what she had just been doing.

"I don't know you. And you don't know me." He started walking again, snapping his fingers to the dog. Andrea rushed to catch up.

"No one wants to know the real Mark Cannon," he said, avoiding her gaze, "and as far as I'm concerned, as long as they give me a chance to do my own thing, then they don't need to know the real me. They can airbrush my photos and doctor my records and change my past if they want, as long as I don't have to go back to being that— that pathetic little boy."

Her skin felt flushed as she took in his impassioned confession. She didn't know what to say. His entire image was built on a foundation of lies—not to mention the kinky sex fetish that he spent a lot of time and effort to keep under wraps. Rodney would kill to get his hands on this inside scoop.

And yet, walking here in the quiet with Mark, his labrador retriever panting alongside them, she wondered once again if she was cut out for her job.

"Let's pretend that kiss didn't happen," Mark said. "It was a mistake."

She shook her head resolutely. Yes, yes she was cut out for her job. Journalism was her first true love. She wouldn't let some handsome face guilt her into keeping the juicy secrets he told her out of her article. That was her real job.

"Um, Andrea?" Mark asked quietly. His brown hair ruffled gently in the breeze and he shook his head as some strands threatened to cover his green eyes.

Andrea looked at his soulful expression, trying not to let herself be swayed by the man standing before her.

He cleared his throat. "I can trust you to keep this conversation just between us, right?"

Andrea felt guilt tear through her very being. The lie that she needed to tell caught in her throat—but she'd lose both of her jobs if she told the truth. And…she'd lose Mark.

"Come on," he said, suddenly all business again. "You can take the plug out when we get back to my place. And next time you wear it, you better ask my permission to orgasm as soon as the feeling starts to hit you, got it?"

Andrea nodded. How had he known? "Got it, Sir."

Wait—*next time?*

CHAPTER THREE

On the set of *Trapped in Action* later that morning, Andrea followed Mark around like the loyal personal assistant she was pretending to be. It seemed to her that most of the time spent on the movie set was spent waiting for something or other.

Between each shot, the camera had to be checked, light readings taken, lights adjusted, makeup fixed, props straightened, cigarettes smoked and lines of dialogue reviewed.

Crew members seemed to stand around a lot. The whole process felt foreign to Andrea and wasn't quite as exciting as she had hoped it would be.

Once the cameras were actually rolling, however, a rush of magic descended over the cast and crew. Mark Cannon was dashing and charming as the movie's hero, and Andrea loved watching him work.

She kept imagining his muscular body pressed against hers, the scent of his enticing, musky cologne making her dizzy with excitement. She kept thinking of his kiss. This man was a real distraction.

If only she had been able to score a cover job as the assistant to a female celebrity, instead of a hot-blooded male. Andrea could be snooping and nosing to her heart's delight, gathering juicy secrets and feeling nothing more than a slight case of uneasiness at the prospect of writing her first big story ever for a tabloid.

She could write about the female celebrity's many love affairs, she could write about cocaine and late-night parties, she could write about eating disorders, either real or imagined.

Andrea sighed. Knowing her, she'd end up accidentally befriending the celebrity and being unable to do her job properly anyhow.

Instead, she was stuck with a ridiculous crush on a man who was only interested in her as a submissive with no strings attached. A man whose secrets filled her with an overwhelming desire to comfort him and cover him in tender kisses, not throw him to the wolves. If only she could learn to have a sense of tabloid journalism. Her loyalty was supposed to be with *The Hollywood Exposer* and with Rodney, in both a professional sense and a romantic sense.

She wouldn't survive as an undercover reporter if she fell for Mark Cannon. Andrea would not let a handsome man run through her life like a whirlwind and break her heart. Andrea had her career and she had Rodney—and if Rodney decided he didn't want her anymore, then someone else would. Hopefully. But now that she'd experienced even a taste of how a dominant man like Mark could make her feel sexually, how could she ever settle for anything less?

Andrea spotted Mark relaxing between takes on one of the elaborately designed sets created on the studio backlot. She walked up to him, trying not to stare at the impressive scene the production designer had created. What looked like part of a huge subway train lay on its side. Fake scorch marks and pieces of jagged metal piercing through the big Plexiglas windows gave the look of a major crash. Andrea noticed they even had shards of shattered glass covering the floor.

"It's actually little pieces of clear rubber," Mark said when he noticed her staring in amazement at the train wreck set. "That way when they shower me with the glass shards I won't get hurt."

Andrea looked up in surprise. "You mean you do your own stunts?"

"As many as they'll let me do. Most movies, they have to switch to showing the back of a stunt double's head every time some action comes along, unless they use CG. It really helps the look of the movie if they can show that I'm the one who's actually doing the stunt."

"Aren't you afraid you'll get hurt, Mark?" she asked, concerned.

Mark grinned. "Why? Are you worried about me?"

Andrea rolled her eyes dramatically. "I don't think so, Sir. You're a big boy, I'm sure you can take care of yourself just fine."

"And what if I can't take care of myself 'just fine'? What if I need a little help?"

"Then that's what I'm here for, Sir," she said, smiling at him despite herself.

"Well, no need to worry too much. The producers wouldn't let me get hurt—they'd lose their investment, you know," Mark said, his tone serious.

* * * * *

Back in his trailer, Mark had to use every bit of self-restraint he could muster just to keep himself from touching Andrea. He wanted to feel her smooth, warm little hand in his. He looked at her delicate fingers as if they held some sort of answer. Her fingernails were short and rounded and the remnants of clear polish covered them, as if she had taken the time to manicure her nails and then got too busy to keep them perfect.

That's my kind of woman, he mused.

Everything about her fascinated him. Her quick sense of humor and her willingness to help him around the movie set. The way his dog had instantly adored her and the way Andrea managed to be the perfect mix of virgin and sexy slut. The way she was trying so very hard to be his perfect submissive, even though she was pretty much failing miserably. That was okay, he was going to enjoy punishing her for her infractions. And kissing her…

Mark looked over at his personal assistant, taking in every detail as she furrowed her thin, black eyebrows in concentration while highlighting his script for today's scenes. Every time he looked at her he had to fight the lust she inspired in him. He wanted to hold her and press his mouth against hers, prodding it gently with his tongue until her sweet bow-shaped lips spread and received him. He wanted to taste her, in an instinctive, animalistic way. Their chaste kiss during his morning hike wasn't enough. He needed more—he needed her. He needed her bound to his bed, kissing his whip, willingly taking his cock in whatever orifice he demanded.

No woman had ever inspired such lust and longing in him before. He didn't understand what it was exactly about Andrea that made her different from all of the other women he had known, but he could feel it in his core.

This woman was special.

* * * * *

Andrea walked past the craft service table, carefully avoiding the tempting goodies that seemed to call out to her from on top of the blue paper tablecloth. Two grips walked by rolling a large piece of equipment, yelling at people in their path to clear the way.

Andrea jumped to the side to avoid a certain death, or at least crushing injury, and slammed right into the last person in the world she wanted to see.

"Rodney—what are you doing here?" she asked in surprise.

A wave of uneasiness passed through her. She knew her sometimes-boyfriend couldn't possibly know the millions of adulterous thoughts that had been floating through her imagination, but she could feel her face registering guilt in spite of herself. Sure, Rodney knew she was playing some sort of spanking game with Mark—presumably for the tabloid and only for the tabloid's sake—but did he know about the rest of it? About the kiss? Could he see it on her face?

"I told security I brought your inhaler," Rodney said.

"I don't have an inhaler. Or asthma."

"What, babe, aren't you glad to see me?" Rodney leaned his gelled head close to Andrea's ear and whispered, "Don't you dare let on that I'm your boss. Today I'm just your boyfriend, visiting you at your new job. Got it?"

Andrea nodded nervously. For a sometimes-boyfriend, he picked the worst times. "Rodney, what if someone recognizes you from the tabloids? You'll blow my cover."

"Don't worry, babe. Leave all the thinking to me as usual, would you?" Rodney threw his arm around Andrea's shoulders and pulled her in for a kiss.

Andrea winced as his thin, dry lips clashed into hers. He smelled like cigarette smoke. At least he hadn't been drinking. He put his hands around her waist.

"Rodney, what on earth do you think you're doing?"

"Andrea, gimme a break. I'm supposed to be your boyfriend. We need some PDA for realism. Kiss me or you're gonna blow *my* cover, babe."

Kissing Rodney had always felt to Andrea as though she were making out with a dead fish. He pressed his lips against hers with such indifference that it left her wanting to cry. But she couldn't very well go out on dates by herself, now could she? Kissing was just part of the deal.

She used to think it was just her, that perhaps she just had a low sex drive. She never was in the mood for romance with Rodney. Dinner and a movie and escaping into the comfort of her own home without giving up more than a few kisses was the best Andrea could hope for when it came to an evening with him.

Now, after meeting Mark Cannon, she suddenly felt a

whole new world of sensation and passion opening up to her—when he spanked her, when he stroked her clit, when he spoke to her in that commanding tone…and especially after he kissed her. And now, her fantasies and the tingle she felt whenever he walked by her were proof enough that she was not doomed to a lifetime of boring, lukewarm sex.

She just knew that if she could feel that way for a man she'd only kissed once, she'd surely be able to recreate those feelings with a man who was at least somewhat attainable. Mark Cannon may be out of reach, but maybe if she tried really hard she could feel with Rodney even an iota of what she felt around Mark.

There was that tingle again…

The man himself suddenly appeared out of nowhere, munching on an apple. He casually strolled over to Andrea and Rodney.

"Ah," Mark said with a tight smile. "Young love. This must be your…"

Mark looked at Andrea quizzically. Andrea hoped the panic wasn't visible in her eyes.

Rodney squeezed Andrea against him and put out his hand to Mark. "Yeah, I'm her boyfriend. I'm just checking up on my girl here to make sure she's not getting in anyone's way," Rodney said. "She has a bad habit of doing that."

The smile on Mark's face never faltered. "Andrea's not in the way. She's pretty good at what she does, so far."

Andrea wanted to die of embarrassment. "Mark," she said stiffly, "this is Rodney Owen. Rodney, Mark Cannon."

Mark acknowledged him with a nod. "So, what do you do, Rodney?"

Rodney's watery brown eyes squinted while he thought up a suitable lie. Andrea elbowed him in the ribs to get him to hurry up. Mark still had that weird smile on his face.

"Rodney doesn't like to tell people about his job," Andrea said. "He knows that nobody likes a used car salesman."

"That's true," Mark said, staring straight at Rodney. "Nobody does."

Andrea's breath caught in her throat. Frannie had spotted them and was walking toward them, holding her two-way radio in one hand. Andrea's pulse quickened in fear. Frannie could blow Rodney's cover with one wrong word.

"Frannie," Andrea said, a little too loudly. "Hi. You remember my boyfriend, Rodney, right?" she asked, urging her friend with her eyes to not breathe a word about Rodney's other position as her boss at the tabloid.

Frannie made a distasteful face in Rodney's general direction. "How could I forget," she said drily. "Um, Mark Cannon?" she turned to Mark with a timidity so unlike her that Andrea almost giggled.

The weird, fake smile that Mark had been wearing just moments before transformed into a genuine smile as he looked down at Frannie. "Just Mark," he said. "You must be Frannie. Andrea mentioned you guys rent a house in the Valley."

Frannie's freckles all but disappeared under the bright red blush that rose in her round cheeks. "Yes—she's the best housemate any one could ask for. It's so great to live with your best friend."

"I bet," Mark said with a wink, and Frannie looked as if she were going to melt into the floor in a puddle of goo.

"Oh my gosh, I almost forgot, I was sent over here to ask you to check in with Wardrobe," Frannie said breathlessly. "They altered your trousers and they needed you for a quick fitting."

Mark glanced at Andrea, her shoulders slumped under the weight of Rodney's arm, and nodded. "Thank you, Frannie. I'm on my way."

He turned to walk off, then turned again and nodded in Rodney's direction. "Rodney," he said. "It was...nice to meet you."

* * * * *

Andrea stood at the tiny sink in Mark's trailer and washed her hands. She felt way too relieved when Rodney had finally gotten the hell out of there. What was he thinking, showing up, acting like her boyfriend, just to see what was happening on the set? Her soapy hands flew up to her mouth and she absentmindedly washed Rodney's unpleasant taste from her lips. She heard the trailer door open and shut behind her and she whirled around, half expecting it to be Rodney again.

It was Mark, though, of course. The trailer was his dressing room, after all. Water dripped down her chin and she grabbed a towel to dry her hands and face but Mark was too quick, stepping toward her, closing the distance between them with one long stride.

"You have a boyfriend?" he asked mildly, taking the towel from her.

Andrea didn't know what to say. She didn't even know what the truth was, really. She just couldn't mention that she worked for Rodney as a tabloid reporter—that was the only truth she knew.

Andrea reached for the towel in Mark's hands, the water dripping down her chin. He held it out of her reach and leaned toward her, flicking his tongue out and licking a droplet off her lips. Andrea's eyes widened in surprise when he patted her face carefully with the soft material. Then he enveloped her wet hands in the towel and held them captive between their bodies.

"What," Mark asked as he looked into her eyes, "would that boyfriend of yours think of this?" He lifted her hands up over her head, pressing his body against hers. Andrea reveled in the feel of his muscular torso through his thin cotton shirt as his face came within inches of hers. "Speak," he said.

"I-I don't know," she said honestly.

Mark held her wrists wrapped tightly in the towel with one of his large hands as he slipped his other hand

44

between them. Andrea gasped as his fingers snaked up under her blouse, touching her bare skin with a featherlight caress.

"You don't know if you have a boyfriend or you don't know what he would think of this?" Mark slid his fingers under her bra and found her left nipple. "Or this?"

Andrea shook her head, unable to speak as he rolled her nipple between his fingers. Suddenly he pinched the hard peak and she moaned.

"Andrea," he breathed, dropping his head to her neck, finally letting her hands fall as well. "Are you, or are you not, available?"

Andrea could barely think straight with all the sensations rushing through her as he licked the pulse on her neck and pulled her shirt down so far that her nipple swelled out of the neckline.

"Yes," she said as he brought his head down to her breast and captured her nipple with his teeth.

His tongue and teeth wreaked havoc on her senses as he continued to tease just the one breast, leaving the other one entirely alone until she found herself practically ripping her shirt off to provide him better access to both of her breasts.

Mark laughed as she let her shirt fall onto the floor of the trailer. "I see," he said. "You want more symmetrical stimulation."

Andrea nodded even though she had no idea what he was talking about. Whatever he wanted to do to her was fine by her.

Mark reached past her to his desk and took two small binder clips off some papers. He pinched her other nipple, which he had left so unloved by his ministrations that the little pink peak wasn't even erect, and attached the clip to it.

Andrea inhaled sharply. The clip pinched hard, keeping a constant pressure that even Mark couldn't maintain with his mouth or fingers. Andrea didn't have to look down to know that both of her nipples were hard enough to cut glass now.

When Mark put the other clip on the nipple he had previously been teasing, Andrea couldn't hold back a moan as the dark pain washed over her. She instinctively brought her hands up to swat the clips away but Mark grabbed them and held them behind her back.

"A few moments, that's all, Andrea. A few moments with your tasty little nipples clamped while you think about whether you really want your so-called boyfriend to keep visiting you on the set."

"I don't want him to visit," Andrea said breathlessly.

Mark swatted her ass with his open palm. "Sir," he reminded her.

"Sir." Andrea's knees felt weak and she swooned as Mark unclamped her nipples and the circulation came rushing back to them along with a new level of erotic pain she had never felt before.

"Drop your pants," he said, letting go of her wrists.

Andrea rushed to obey him, wriggling as she lowered her jeans. Would he spank her again?

Mark dipped his hand down the front of her panties and slid his finger across her clit. "You're wet," he said with a smile. "If I can get you wet just by playing with those nipples of yours, I wonder what I can do to you when I have you tied up, with your spread pussy at my mercy?"

Andrea swallowed. "I-I don't know, Sir."

"At some point, Andrea, we're going to have to find out."

* * * * *

A few days later, Andrea sat at the little desk in Mark's trailer contemplating the best way to start with his abundance of fan mail. She had to keep shifting in the hard seat since her ass was still sore from all the spankings Mark had been giving her. No wonder his assistants didn't last long—especially if they weren't made aware up front, like she had been, that getting a spanking for being ten minutes late was actually part of the job.

Now she had more work to do, and her ass couldn't handle Mark coming in to his trailer to discover that she'd been procrastinating. Andrea promised herself she would take care of all the fan mail before she gave in to her burning curiosity and opened his personal mail—that one envelope that had been addressed to his home address.

Mark had laughed at her look of bewilderment when he had asked her to answer his mail. Silly of her to think he might have time for something as mundane as writing letters. She guessed it just wasn't glamorous enough for a movie star to deal with.

Well, someone had to do it and, she admitted to herself, she was glad for the opportunity to delve into his personal mail. She knew she was just avoiding doing the tedious parts of it, although Mark had told her that she wouldn't be stuck reading and hand-writing responses to each individual piece of fan mail.

While the process seemed rather impersonal to Andrea, she knew that the only way she'd be able to answer them all was just to start. Sighing, she pulled one envelope from the pile and opened it.

Dear Mark Cannon!! I love you, I love you, you are so cute, you are the best action hero ever in the whole world and will you come to my third grade class for show-and-tell next week please!!!
Yours Truly, Nina S.

Andrea smiled at the innocence of the young fan. She typed Nina S.'s name into a form letter, printed it out, and stamped the bottom with a custom-made stamp that bore Mark Cannon's squiggly autograph.

Only an hour later, Andrea's fingers began to ache and she had more paper cuts than she could handle. The mysterious envelope addressed to Mark's home address sat to the side just begging to be opened.

She could open it now, she reasoned, and if he questioned her about it, she could fib and say it had gotten mixed in with the fan mail and she had opened it without noticing his home address. Andrea tossed the letter into the pile of mail and shuffled the papers a bit, so that her fib could become a half-fib.

The twinge of guilt let her know her tabloid-journalist mentality was in danger. Damn it.

She opened the envelope. It was a single piece of stationary, folded around a wallet-size photograph. It was a handwritten note, in a woman's delicate cursive handwriting.

Mark—sweetheart—I haven't seen you in almost a year. Our little apartment just isn't a home without you in it. I love you. xoxo—K

Andrea picked up the photo gingerly, as if it might burn her fingers. It was a picture of Mark, wearing a baseball cap and smiling into the face of a tiny baby wrapped in a pink blanket. Andrea turned the photo over in amazement. The same cursive handwriting was etched across the back—four simple words.

She misses you, Mark.

Andrea gasped and dropped the photo. Her hands shook as she knelt to pick it up. Was Mark a father? Did he have a secret lover? Maybe even an abandoned wife and child? And here she was, playing sex games with him.

She felt as if her skin had grown tight around her. She struggled to take a calm, deep breath, tried to tell herself it shouldn't matter if Mark had a special someone. A little family tucked away from the limelight. Of course he did. Did she really think a man like Mark Cannon would go through life without breaking a few hearts? He probably had a jilted lover in every state. Maybe even more illegitimate children. That's why he said kissing her was a mistake—he could probably rationalize spanking his personal assistant, or toying with her, even rubbing her clit, but the kiss was just too personal.

Rodney would be ecstatic when she called him with the news that Mark had even more skeletons in his closet than a spanking fetish.

So why did she feel so awful about it?

CHAPTER FOUR

Rodney's voice grated through the phone line, scraping Andrea's very last nerve. She sat on the edge of her bed, twisting the phone cord. Peppers lay next to her, unaware of his owner's distress.

"Andrea, babe, it's been a week and a freaking half now," Rodney said. "What the hell are you doing over there on that movie set that's taking so long?"

"Rodney, I'm sorry, I just think I need some more time," Andrea said for the hundredth time in the past twenty minutes.

"You mean to tell me that you've been Mark Cannon's personal assistant, walking his stupid dog, buying his stupid lattes and running all his stupid errands and you don't have enough spanking stories or whatever for me?"

"I'm sorry, Rodney, it's not that, per se, it's just that I need more time to get all my facts straight so I can weave them all together into a really shocking exposé."

"You need time to get your facts straight? Babe, who do you think you work for? *The Los Angeles* friggin' *Times*?"

Andrea sighed. She knew this would happen. If only she could tell Rodney about some of the delicious secrets she had discovered about Mark Cannon, action star. But every time she opened her mouth to tell Rodney that she had indeed been doing her job as an undercover tabloid journalist, the thought of how crushed Mark would be if he found out about her betrayal filled her with guilt.

Andrea knew that her insane schoolgirl crush on Mark was partly to blame. She knew he would never be interested in her, not in a forever type of way. Even if he were, he was a heartbreaker. A playboy.

Mark Cannon was not someone who could ever return even an inkling of what she was beginning to feel for him. It was up to her to put an end to her ridiculous fantasizing right away, before it destroyed the career she had been working for her whole life, not to mention the one relationship that actually had a chance of existing in her lifetime—with Rodney.

After this past phone call, the thought of going on a date with Rodney didn't sound like something she wanted to do, but it suddenly occurred to Andrea that a night out with Rodney might be the perfect antidote to her feelings for Mark.

"Hey…Rodney?" Andrea said. "Do you miss me?"

Rodney's voice softened slightly at her switch from "Work Andrea" to "Girlfriend Andrea".

"Of course I miss you, babe," Rodney said. "Coffee's not the same unless it's you making it."

"So, did you want to go out for drinks, maybe? We haven't even seen each other since you visited me on the set."

Rodney's cruel laugh shocked her. "Andrea, seriously," he said. "I wasn't 'visiting you'. I was scoping out possible stories for the paper. The next time you see me, you better have Mark Cannon's very soul written in two-inch-high letters and ready for publication in *The Exposer*."

Andrea slammed the phone down in humiliation and anger. Why did she even try with Rodney? She didn't even *like* him. And it was becoming painfully clear that he didn't like her either. He only went out with her out of pity. Or because he wanted something. Or maybe he was just bored.

Peppers meowed grumpily at her, annoyed she had disturbed his catnap.

Hot, wet tears welled up in her eyes and she brushed them away hurriedly with the back of her hand. She caught a glimpse of herself in the mirror in her bedroom and wailed in frustration. Streaks of mascara ran down her pale face.

Just look at her—it was no wonder no man ever felt anything for her. If she couldn't even get a rather average man like Rodney to like her, how could she even think that an incredible person like Mark Cannon would want her?

Ring! Ring! The phone's shrill cry snapped Andrea back out of her puddle of self-pity.

"What do you want?" she answered stiffly.

"Hmm," a deep baritone replied. "Do I get to choose anything at all, or are there limits?"

"Mark—oh my gosh. I'm sorry, I thought it was someone else," Andrea said, embarrassed.

"No problem." Mark laughed.

Andrea took a deep breath and tried to compose herself. "What can I do for you, Mark? There are, um, no limits."

"Prove it. Come over."

Smiling at the phone, she said, "I'm on my way, Sir."

* * * * *

On the way to Mark's house, Andrea got a text from him, telling her to let herself in and go to his bedroom and undress.

She slowly opened the big front door, taking a moment to notice a bunch of new photos spread out on the little table under the mirror in the grand foyer. Publicity shots, probably there for Mark to sign off on. She picked up one of him with a popular child actress whose name escaped her. Probably nerves—she was about to go undress and do heaven knows what with Mark. In that publicity shot,

Mark looked as if he'd be such a good father. His face looked so sincere as he smiled at the little girl with loving kindness.

Then again, he was an actor. He got paid millions of dollars to look sincere.

But what about the photo of Mark smiling down at that little baby? What about that note?

(*She misses you, Mark.*)

Andrea wondered if that could really be Mark's child. The letter that came with the photo certainly seemed to suggest that was the case. Could she really feel so strongly for a man who might have abandoned another woman? Abandoned a baby? She didn't know all the facts. She shouldn't jump to conclusions, it wouldn't be fair to her or to Mark. There could be other elements in play here.

Andrea sighed. She could spend all night beating herself up over this, or she could get the courage to walk up those stairs and get naked. She put the photo down.

* * * * *

Mark laughed as his cell phone buzzed. She had texted him that she was ready for him. Cute. Mark walked into his bedroom and saw Andrea, completely and utterly naked, for the first time. His breath caught in his throat and he shook his head to clear his thoughts.

So what if she was beautiful? He'd met tons of beautiful women in his life.

So what if she was also kind and funny and hard-working? So what if his dog adored her? So what if she had managed to learn more about him in the past couple of weeks than he'd ever let anyone else discover in a lifetime? So what if he couldn't stop fantasizing about kissing her again—about doing a lot more than kissing…

There was a reason Mark didn't allow himself to date while shooting a movie. Women were a distraction. He needed to devote all of his energy to his craft. The studio was paying him an obscene amount of money to deliver what was expected of him. If he failed, his career could be over sooner than he could say "has-been".

He had worked too long and too hard to let some woman rush into his life and ruin everything. He just couldn't understand why this particular woman was proving to be so hard to ignore. He wanted an assistant who wouldn't mind a spanking here and there—but he hadn't planned on taking on the responsibility of initiating a woman into the pleasures of BDSM play.

And yet he had practically begged her for the chance to do exactly that.

"Open the closet door and pick something," he said.

Andrea looked at him nervously but did as he asked. He wanted to teach her a lesson in submission, and the best way to guarantee her willingness to participate was to have her pick her own punishment. She had an array of paddles and whips to choose from.

* * * * *

Andrea peered into the closet. What did he mean, pick something? She gasped as she saw the wall covered with various paddles, whips, ropes, some handcuffs, some sort of bar with fuzzy cuffs at the end and a bunch of sex toys, most of which she had never known existed.

Part of her was tempted to pick nothing at all, but as she looked back over her shoulder at Mark, she knew that what she really wanted was for him to show her what this was all about.

She liked the spanking, so...she picked a paddle. It looked harmless enough. She walked up and handed it to him. He was still fully dressed, which made her feel even more naked, somehow.

"Good choice," he said. "Lean over the bed."

She leaned over, bracing her forearms on the expensive comforter and taking a deep breath.

Nothing happened.

Suddenly she felt his hand caress her ass, softly. Then the paddle slapped her ass cheek so hard that she fell forward.

"Get up, gorgeous," he said.

She put herself back in position and the paddle came down again, then again, causing her to gasp with each smack. Her skin felt warm and flushed. He stopped and she inhaled sharply as she felt his long fingers test her pussy. She knew she was wet, she couldn't help it.

"You want more?" he asked.

"Yes Sir," she said.

She felt the thick handle of the paddle press against her pussy and he slid it deep inside her, thrusting slowly as she pressed back against it. Suddenly it was out and she was still moving her hips, desperate for more. The paddle slapped her ass again, so hard that she knew now that he had been testing her before. He kept going, a steady rain of blows until she was tempted to cry out for him to give her a moment to catch her breath—and then it stopped.

Mark picked her up bodily and set her gently on the bed. "Spread your legs," he said.

She did, her ass burning uncomfortably as she lay on the inflamed skin. He walked back over to the closet and rummaged around, coming out with a thin riding crop that ended with a flap of leather.

It was small, how bad could it be?

"Don't move," he warned. "I promise I won't do anything that will harm you."

Andrea fought her natural instinct to close her legs as he softly slapped the leather against her labia. It actually didn't hurt at all, it just woke up her nerve endings, reminding her how much she wanted him there, right where he was prodding with his fingertips, spreading her nether lips, leaving her clit exposed.

Thwack! The leather square hit her directly on her clit and she squealed, her knees shutting against her best intentions to keep them open.

"You're new at this, so you don't have the control you should," he said. "For now I'll be happy to help you with that, if you're willing. May I restrain you?"

Andrea nodded, grateful that she wouldn't have to try to keep her own legs open. "Yes Sir."

Again Mark went into the closet, this time returning to the bed with some silk cords. He tied a loop around each of her knees and pulled them far apart, securing them under the bedframe. Next he tied her hands above her head to the headboard. She felt completely open, exposed…and more turned-on than she had ever been before in her admittedly limited sexual experience.

"Let's test those bonds," he said as he gently slapped her clit with the crop again. Her knees jerked in her bonds, trying to close despite her efforts to keep them open, but they were held firmly apart by the silk cords. To her embarrassment, her arms also jerked as she tried to lower her hands to protect her sensitive pussy. She couldn't.

"I love your breasts," he murmured as he brought the crop down first on one nipple, then the other. She gasped as her nipples immediately grew hard and red. "Beautiful little nipples." He smacked them again playfully before reaching down and pinching them, rolling them in his fingers until she was moaning. "Beautiful pussy." The crop hit her clit again, harder this time, then again twice more in rapid succession.

Her clit was burning, swollen—and then he pulled out a vibrator. "Do you have a vibrator, Andrea?"

"N-no Sir."

"Whyever not?" He turned it on and the buzzing sound both terrified and excited her. She almost came the second he pressed it against her clit but then he pulled it away.

"Remember what I told you about asking permission to come?" He pressed it against her clit again, turning up the speed until she came instantly, moaning loudly, unable to help herself. Mark just laughed. "I thought you might do that. Do you know what the punishment is for naughty little pussies who come without permission?"

Andrea shook her head. Another spanking, perhaps?

Mark smiled. "The punishment for naughty pussies

who come without permission is called torture orgasms, and I think that is just what the doctor ordered for you." He pressed the vibrator against her clit again.

"Please, Mark, may I come?" she begged as she felt the sensation rising in her again.

"Not only may you come, but now you no longer have the option of *not* coming. That's why they're called torture orgasms. I'm going to keep going until you've reached your orgasm limit, and the only way to find out what your personal orgasm limit is just to keep pushing you. Then push some more. Then, just for fun—my fun, that is—I'm going to torture your pretty little clit with some more."

Andrea could barely respond as another orgasm hit her, this one sharper and more intense than before. Last time he had removed the vibrator for a moment, giving her time to recover a bit before rubbing her clit with the vibrator some more. But this time—as soon as she came he held the vibrator steady despite her frantic twisting in her ropes to get away. The overstimulation was insane and she cried out as she came again.

"Please, Mark," she begged.

He didn't let up—he merely dipped his fingers in her pussy, and when they came out wet and slippery, he smiled and continued. "Your body can't lie."

CHAPTER FIVE

Later that evening, Mark and Andrea sat next to each other on the high stools at the granite countertop in his kitchen. He hadn't said a word in the past three minutes, enjoying the companionable silence. He never clammed up around anyone, but it was suddenly becoming clear to him that Andrea was not just any girl. She liked him—the real him, not just the image she had of him. It was a new, strange feeling.

Mark looked at her and shrugged, smiling. He wanted to tell her that he knew most people only liked him because he was famous. Some people hated him without knowing him because he was famous.

Everyone, from the kid who made his lattes to the mailman and even his own cousins, acted differently around him once he became a movie star.

Mark could tell that every word he said was being remembered for use in a story to tell friends later. If a piece of trash fell from his pocket onto the sidewalk, before he could pick it up the paparazzi were there to snap a photo and label him a litterbug in the next morning's headlines.

Mark wanted to tell Andrea all of this, but he knew

he'd just end up sounding like an ungrateful, "woe-is-me" type. He wanted to tell Andrea that the reason his evening with her was so special to him was because it felt as if she liked being with him even though she didn't need to be.

That felt nice. To be liked for just being himself.

It seemed that once he became a celebrity, no one could ever really care about the real Mark Cannon. He had felt that he had better get used to people only liking him for his fame and money, because so far, that was the best he could get.

Now things were looking up.

* * * * *

Frannie's jaw nearly dropped to the floor. "Oh my gosh," she said. "You're not serious." Her morning cup of coffee sloshed onto the kitchen table as she gestured with her hands.

Andrea sighed and collapsed into the straight-backed wooden chair next to her friend. "I know. I can't believe it either. I'm such an idiot." Andrea groaned and dropped her face into her hands.

"Um, Andrea? Fill me in here. You got to hook up with Mark Cannon, for goodness sake. What's the problem?"

"You don't get it, Frannie. We didn't have sex exactly, but I basically cheated on Rodney, and I, uh…had fun with Mark even though I know I have ulterior motives. That's not cool."

"You never get to have that kind of exciting experience with Rodney," Frannie said. "You deserved to have some fun." She nibbled on her lower lip. "Does Mark know that you're working for the tabloid?"

"No. No way. He would have said something."

"As much as I hate the idea of you smearing Mark Cannon, you did say you weren't going to let him get in the way of your career at the tabloid," Frannie said, reaching down to pet Peppers as he strolled past the table, rubbing his furry little face against Andrea's shin.

Andrea stood, causing Peppers to scurry away. "I did

say that, didn't I? I can't give up this opportunity by letting some good-looking—okay, great-looking—celebrity get in my way. I just know I can find a way to turn this around to my advantage. Maybe I should just throw my morals away and get started on my article—I still have my scathing exposé to write for Rodney."

Frannie looked at her friend warily. "Don't do anything you're going to regret, Andrea."

Andrea looked back at Frannie. "What's to regret? I took the position as Mark's personal assistant because I want to be a journalist. Now I finally have a chance to make a career for myself at *The Hollywood Exposer*. And you know what? I'm going to take that chance if it kills me."

Andrea sat back down in her chair defiantly.

It's not going to kill me, she realized. People don't really die of a broken heart, do they?

* * * * *

The afternoon sun filtered in through the little window in Mark's trailer, crossing slices of light across the script Andrea was highlighting. The dialogue had just been rewritten that morning, and Mark stood over Andrea's shoulder, looking at the new material.

"Can I flip the page, Sir?" Andrea asked.

Mark's head was so close to hers that she could feel the air move slightly as he nodded. "Andrea?" he said softly.

"Uh huh?" she murmured, her teeth nibbling on the end of the neon yellow highlighter.

"Can you run lines with me? I'm supposed to be ready to shoot this thing tonight," he said.

He was so physically close, leaning over her shoulder like that. His breath was hot on the back of her neck. She turned around and found his face only inches away.

"Um…yeah, I can run lines with you." His proximity made her want him so much that it took every bit of her willpower to slowly stand and take a step back.

Mark looked down at his script to read the line of dialogue, then looked up at her. Andrea was surprised by the sudden change in him. He seemed…different.

"Mark?" she asked, unsure of what was expected of her.

He grinned at her. "Not Mark. I'm trying to get into character now. Pretend I'm just a tough action hero with a heart of gold," he said, laughing. "I've got my lines memorized, just follow along and read the part of the leading lady," he said, pointing to her script.

"I'll try my best, Sir. But I should warn you, I got a C in my college drama class," Andrea admitted.

Mark looked at her, and once again he had subtly changed into his role. "Don't move an inch," he whispered with controlled panic in his voice. "You'll set off the tripwire and blow up the entire building."

Andrea looked down at the script, reading her line, trying to put as much realism into her character as her limited acting skills would allow. "I need you to slide under the laser beam and decode the combination!"

Mark looked at her. "I can't do it," he said. "If only I could remember what the Tibetan monk told me about inner strength." He spoke with the deliberate intensity of his character.

"You can do it. You've already saved the world twice today. Just do it once more, that's all I ask." Andrea read the dialogue with a barely contained smirk. "Mark, I'm sorry," she said, laughing. "This dialogue is rather…"

Mark stepped closer to her. "You think it's a silly scene, huh?" He smiled.

Andrea blushed. He was so close to her that she couldn't think straight. Whatever happened to her using her time with him to get the scoop for her real job?

"I don't really know anything about movies. You'll take this wooden dialogue and make it fly off the page. You're a really good actor," she said quietly. Her face felt hot and flushed.

"I thought you didn't know anything about movies." He stepped toward her, pressing his strong, muscular body against her.

She inhaled sharply, dizzy from his very nearness. He was at least a head taller than her, and she had to tilt her head up to look at his clear green eyes.

"Andrea," he whispered. He ran his hand through her hair and she reveled in the feel of his fingers. He brushed his lips against hers.

She moaned softly and let her hand slide up the hard muscles of his back, feeling them ripple underneath his T-shirt, tense and then relax as she worked her hands over his skin.

He pressed his lips against hers, spreading hers slowly with his tongue. She parted to receive him, her tongue dancing with his inside her mouth.

Andrea sipped at Mark's full lower lip, nibbling it as she tasted his kiss. She could feel his cock, hard and thick, pressing against her and her heartbeat quickened.

She leaned against his body, letting the pressure build as they held each other, kissing deeply. He caressed her face as he held her so close she could breathe in his incredible scent.

"Mark," she said softly, brushing his lips with hers.

She wasn't sure what she wanted to say. *How strange,* she thought. When he kissed her that morning in the Hollywood Hills, it was so unexpected, so sudden, she barely had time to register that he was kissing her before he had abruptly pulled away. And the other night at his house, they had been so playful, so sexual, without any real tenderness. Tenderness hadn't felt necessary then.

But this kiss…this kiss was with the Mark she was truly beginning to know. The personal bond that had been building between them made the kiss more incredible, more special than any she had ever experienced.

Mark's gaze seemed to penetrate her. "You have blue eyes," he said, as if he were noticing for the first time. "And that was a nice kiss."

Andrea nodded, swallowing hard. "It was nice."

"I need more," he said, bending his face down to nibble on her earlobe. "I need you."

His hands went up under the back of her blouse, and she raised her arms to help him take it off. He lifted her off her feet and laid her on the cot, tugging her jeans off as he kissed her so deeply she was scarcely aware of the fact that he was now naked too.

She stroked her hands over his broad chest, outlining his muscles with her palms.

"I've wanted this since the moment I laid eyes on you," he murmured. He caressed her breasts and she shivered with anticipation.

"Andrea, please spread your legs," he said. "I want to fuck you. No—I want to make love to you. May I?"

"Yes Sir," she breathed, opening her legs as wide as they would go.

He lay on top of her and she relished the feel of his weight restraining her. He fumbled with a condom, and then with one slow thrust he was inside her, hitting her G-spot with such a slow, tender motion that her orgasm began building within minutes.

"Damn, you feel so good." He moved within her as if he had become a part of her.

She ran her fingers through his thick brown hair and grasped at his broad shoulders as he took her to a dizzying place she had never been before.

She cried out as a wave of sensation rushed over her and he held her tightly until a low moan escaped his lips and his thrusts deepened, plunging into her so hard and fast that her orgasm kept moving through her. Finally he collapsed on top of her, kissing her fiercely.

He lifted his head. "I don't know why I've been fighting for so long to not do that."

"Don't worry," Andrea smiled. "I'll try not to sue you for sexual harassment."

He laughed and rolled off her, lying on his back with one hand tucked under the pillow. "Give me a minute and

I'll be good to go again." He slid the used condom off his wilting cock and tossed it into the wastebasket.

"Again?"

Mark rolled back onto her and lifted her hands high above her head, pinning her down. "I'm going to rape you this time," he said.

Andrea's eyes widened.

"Not really," he whispered, smiling. "If you're not into it just say, 'safeword' and I'll stop. But if you want me, you can fight back as much as you like and I'll keep right on fucking you."

Andrea smiled—no way she was using a safeword when she absolutely wanted to be taken. She warmed up to the idea of playful resistance as she tried to free herself from his strong hands but it felt as if her wrists were encased in iron shackles instead of Mark's hands.

She twisted her body, trying to get out from under him, but his weight pinned her down. She wasn't going anywhere—and her "resisting" had indeed given Mark an erection. She tried to close her legs but he kept them spread with his own legs. A sheen of perspiration covered her as she got into the game, struggling against him and loving every second of losing the fight.

She got so into it she barely noticed when he sheathed himself again. He pressed his cock into her pussy and thrust in and out of her deeply, keeping her hands pinned above her head.

"Come for me, Andrea. Now."

She didn't have to be told twice. Mark uttered a deep guttural sound as he came, his cock twitching inside her. He released her hands and pulled out, quickly tying off the condom and cleaning up as Andrea lay on the cot, boneless and thoroughly satiated.

Then his eyebrows furrowed.

Mark's forehead crinkled as if in confusion. He seemed to be looking across the room. Andrea turned her head, following his gaze.

"Mark? What's wrong?"

Mark slowly untangled his arms from her embrace and stood, pulling on his jeans. He stepped toward the corner of the trailer, near his desk.

And then she saw it. A single piece of pink paper, removed from its white envelope, was lying on the floor beneath the desk.

"I know that stationery…" he murmured under his breath, plucking the note off the floor, revealing the photo that lay beneath it.

Andrea knew what the letter said without looking at it—the words were etched into her memory. It was just a simple handwritten note, in a woman's delicate cursive handwriting. *Mark—sweetheart—I haven't seen you in almost a year…*

Mark's face looked pained. He picked the photo of himself holding the baby off the floor and placed it on the desk. He turned to Andrea, holding the note in his hand gingerly, as if it might burn him.

"Andrea, where did this come from?"

A chill ran down her spine as she gathered her clothing from the floor and dressed quickly. "I-I'm sorry, Mark. I think it came from New York."

"That's not what I meant, Andrea," he said slowly. "This is a personal letter for my eyes only. Did you open it? Why was it on the floor?"

Andrea's face felt tight. Hot tears filled her eyes and threatened to spill over her flushed cheeks. "I opened it," she said.

She wished she had the ability to lie and just tell him that it had been an accident, that it had been mixed in with his fan mail, but it was no use. She couldn't look at the man she had just made love to and make up a story. It wouldn't matter even if she could follow her original plan and lie, she could tell by the look on his face that he already knew the truth.

"It was a real person who wrote this letter to me.

66

Someone who cares deeply about whether or not I respond. Were you ever planning on telling me about this?" Mark asked.

Andrea couldn't contain the rush of tears that covered her face. She wiped them away with the back of her hand. She had made a big mistake. How could she ever think she was cut out for a job like this?

"I'm so sorry, Mark," she said. "I wasn't sure who it was from or what it was about, and I guess I thought I needed some time to look into it. I feel horrible about this."

Mark stared at her, his face unreadable. "Look into it? What the hell does that mean?"

Andrea picked up her purse and stepped out of the trailer door. "I'm sorry."

"Don't walk away," he said.

Andrea turned in the doorway and looked at him. "I don't know what else to do."

"Why don't you come back inside, sit down, and explain to me why you didn't tell me about this letter."

Andrea bit her lip. Her stomach was in knots and she felt so miserable about her situation that she thought she might throw up.

"I don't know why I did it, Sir," she said. "I have no excuse. I guess I read that note and felt uncomfortable learning so much about your personal life. There's information there that you obviously weren't ready or willing to share with me," she said, avoiding his gaze.

"Andrea," he said, tilting her chin up so that she was forced to look into his eyes. "What exactly do you think you learned about me from that note?"

"Well," she said slowly, "You've left someone, someone who is still in love with you. A woman that you lived with, maybe even were married to. You've left behind a baby. A little girl who misses you, according to the note on the back of the photo. And I know that this isn't just some crazy fan, or someone delusional. Because she mailed the letter to your home address, and it was a photo of you holding that child." She struggled to keep her expression from betraying her conflicting emotions.

Andrea looked at Mark's handsome face. A tiny muscle in his jaw flexed, as if his jaw was clenched in concentration.

He walked over to his desk and picked up the photo of the baby. "She's beautiful, isn't she?" he asked, his eyes moist. "It's been too long since I've been home. I get carried away with work, and with the whole lifestyle out here in La-La-Land."

Andrea didn't know what to say. She sat down on the cot in his trailer and waited for him to explain.

"I've got a few days off next week while they shoot some establishing shots that don't involve me," he said. "I'm booking a flight to New York. I need to go home and visit."

Hot tears filled Andrea's eyes for what felt like the tenth time that day. He was leaving, and she had forced his hand.

"I'm sorry you have to leave, but I know that it's what's right," she said. "A man should be with his family."

"Yes," Mark said firmly. "Which means I'm taking a little trip. I'd like you to come with me, Andrea."

"What?" she asked incredulously. "Why would you want me to join you on such a personal excursion?"

"Because you're my personal assistant."

Andrea looked at him in confusion. "I don't understand, Sir."

Mark's thick eyebrows knitted together. "Well, there's something I don't understand," he said. "Why did you just sleep with me if you think I'm a man who abandoned his wife and child? Why are you still here if you're under the impression that I'm a deadbeat dad?"

"I-I didn't have all my facts straight yet. I didn't want to jump to conclusions. Plus, you didn't seem like the type to just abandon a family. I thought there might be deeper reasons behind it that I couldn't understand with my limited information."

Mark's brow slowly relaxed. "Thank you for believing in me," he said. "This is not my daughter," he said, pointing to the picture of the baby.

"It's not?" Andrea asked, surprising herself with the relief she felt. He wasn't a deadbeat dad.

"She's my niece. My older sister lives with her husband, the baby and my mother in New York City. And I haven't been home to visit in way too long," he said. "I'd like you to join me in New York—and I want you to do it because you want to, not just as my assistant."

* * * * *

Andrea practically floated home, she was so excited. Peppers meowed loudly as soon as she walked in the door, milling around the kitchen in his not-so-subtle hungry cat dance.

"Okay, Peppers, calm down, sweetie," she said, opening a can of cat food and spooning it into his dish.

Frannie walked in the door, her cheeks rosy from the evening air. "Andrea," she greeted, flopping down on the couch in the living room. "I feel like we're working on different movie sets. I never get to see you."

"I know," Andrea said. "Is there any chance you could watch Peppers this weekend?"

Frannie raised an eyebrow. "I could. Dare I ask why?"

Andrea sat down next to Frannie, trying to act casual, even though she knew from the looks her roommate was giving her that she was failing miserably.

"It's no big deal, it's just…Mark invited me to meet his family in New York City."

"Oh my gosh!" Frannie squealed, hugged Andrea and squealed some more.

Andrea laughed, giddy with excitement. "I know, can you believe it?"

Suddenly Frannie's face dropped. "Oh no, Andrea, are you gonna use this as fuel for your exposé on him? You're not going to drag Mark Cannon's family into this, are you?"

"No, no. But I should tell Rodney that I'm going. He'd fire me for sure if he found out from the grapevine." Andrea eyed the phone, worried. "Oh man, I guess that means I should call Rodney right now, huh?"

Frannie shook her head vehemently. "No—don't tell that jerk. You don't still think of him as your boyfriend, do you?"

Andrea shook her head slowly. "No, I guess Rodney is not my 'sometimes boyfriend' anymore. He basically said as much the last time we spoke—which is why I feel comfortable getting to know Mark on a more personal level."

"So don't call him. What Rodney doesn't know can't hurt him."

"He's still my boss, Frannie. And what Rodney doesn't know can hurt me if he finds out I'm off with my journalistic subject on a pleasure trip."

Frannie frowned. "Fine, tell Rodney. Maybe even take some notes during your trip or something for appearance's sake. Just don't mess up this opportunity with Mark—he obviously wants to get to know you better."

"All right," Andrea said. "Pass me the cordless, please, and I'll just get it done with now."

Frannie grabbed the phone and handed it to Andrea wordlessly.

Andrea dialed Rodney's cell phone number from memory, her pulse racing. The line rang only twice before her boss picked up.

"This is Rodney," he said, sounding bored.

"Rodney, hi. Andrea here," she said, willing herself to sound normal.

"I don't know any Andrea," Rodney said, a tinge of attitude sharpening his voice.

"Um? Rodney? It's Andrea Landley."

"Oh, you mean the woman who wants to be a tabloid

journalist at *The Hollywood Exposer* but refuses to actually do her job? That Andrea Landley?"

"Rodney, don't do this."

"Don't do what, Andrea?" he said. "I can't do a thing around here with all the higher-ups barraging me with memos regarding how I'm going to fill next week's tabloid."

"I know, and I'm sorry for that. Maybe I can write a small filler piece on somebody else until I get my notes together on Mark Cannon," Andrea suggested hopefully.

"I can't even trust you to write filler, Andrea. You begged me to give you this shot, and the only reason I gave it to you is because you've got access to Mark Cannon and his sex fetish thingy. But you know what? You don't have what it takes to succeed as a tabloid journalist."

"Yes, I do, Rodney. It's always been my dream to be a reporter," she said. "I don't want to be your secretary forever."

"Well, that's good, because you're not even a very good secretary. You obviously are completely incompetent. Anyone else would have spent a few days gathering intel, gotten a few kinky spanking scenarios under their belt, and they'd be done and writing about it by now. You've stuck around with him for some reason. Why?"

"There are potential stories coming out of this, Rodney," she said. "I just need a little more time."

Rodney snorted. "You're not an undercover tabloid reporter pretending to be Mark Cannon's personal assistant. You've become Mark Cannon's assistant, pretending to be a tabloid reporter."

Andrea exhaled loudly in frustration. "Rodney, listen to me. Mark is taking me with him to visit his family in New York for the week."

She heard him snort. "Why?"

"Because his sister sent him a really nice letter that reminded him how much he's missing," Andrea said, trailing her finger over the worn couch cover. "I mean, he hasn't seen them in almost a year so it makes sense that he'd want to visit."

"You know, this could be really good. Stop by my office and I'll fit you with a wire."

"A wire?" Andrea repeated, confused.

"Now's the time to prove you are committed to your career. You're not really going to let some movie star who will probably forget your name by the end of the month keep you from success, are you?"

Andrea looked over at her roommate sitting on the couch, watching her expectantly.

Frannie mouthed, "What's he want?" Concern creased her forehead.

Andrea shook her head. "I don't know what to do, Rodney," she said quietly, hating how timid she must sound to her ex.

"Just come stop by *The Exposer* and pick up your wire. Let me show you how to record the things Mark Cannon wants to do with you," Rodney said.

"Rodney…"

"Whatever. Figure out what you want to do on your way over to my office."

"What do you mean, figure out what I want to do?" Andrea asked.

Rodney sighed into the phone. "Either wear a wire and write the story for me, or you're fired, Andrea. Not only will you not be my secretary anymore, but you will never be a journalist. You'll be done. Blacklisted. Get it?"

Andrea frowned as she heard the line disconnect. She silently picked up her purse and headed for the front door.

Frannie jumped up from the couch. "Where are you going?"

"To Rodney's office," she said simply, and walked out the door.

CHAPTER SIX

Mark tried to relax as he let the jets from the Jacuzzi pulse against his lower back. He looked up at the night sky, grateful for the privacy the palm trees afforded his backyard.

He couldn't stop thinking about how Andrea felt writhing underneath him, making love to him...even though he knew he should try to think objectively about the whole situation. Andrea had let her curiosity get the best of her and she'd read that letter from his sister. Mark wondered why he wasn't as outraged as he'd expected to be.

Maybe it was because Andrea wasn't a stranger anymore. Maybe it was because he wanted to share things with her—things he never talked about with anyone else.

Why didn't Andrea just tell him that she'd seen the letter and the photo? He remembered the look on her face when she tried to explain her actions to him.

Her blue eyes had looked clear and glassy with tears— and she had looked so beautiful it was all he could do not to wrap her in his arms and kiss her tears away. And then spank the hell out of her for getting him all worked up.

Remembering her sincere regret and apologies, Mark

realized that Andrea's fear that Mark might be a deadbeat dad had paralyzed her from taking immediate action with that note. She hadn't handled the situation perfectly, but at least she stayed to talk about it when he asked her not to leave.

Mark was amazed that he'd met a woman who'd seen him fall off his pedestal and still stuck around to help him stand up again. Andrea knew Mark was not perfect and yet she still didn't walk out that trailer door.

Having that support made him want to have her by his side when he went home to New York. He knew he had to make the trip, but going home always left him feeling empty and depressed. Seeing how happy his sister and her husband were with their baby and their little apartment in the city made Mark question his lifestyle. Money, fame and women who dated him for a taste of the good life were all he had to show for his celebrity status.

Mark wondered how important that would all be to him on his deathbed, as he looked back on his life.

Would he look at his résumé and list of movie credits and feel fulfilled? Would he remember the one-night stands and late-night parties with a smile?

Mark shook his head, stepping slowly out of the hot tub, letting the warm Southern California air caress his wet body.

"When I look back on my life," he whispered, "I want something real to show for it."

The image of Andrea's soft, warm lips melting into his kiss sent a shiver through his body that had nothing to do with the breeze. He wanted to take her long dark hair and run his fingers through it, letting the strands fall loosely around her beautiful face. He wanted to have access to her body whenever he needed to be with her, which lately felt like all the time.

Andrea's bow-shaped mouth had fit perfectly underneath his lips, and Mark longed to taste that strawberry lip gloss on her sweet little mouth once more.

* * * * *

Andrea pushed open the heavy metal door to *The Hollywood Exposer* headquarters slowly, dreading her meeting with Rodney. She smoothed a disobedient lock of hair out of her eyes and wiped her hands on her jeans. She wished she'd taken the time to dress more professionally before she'd run out the door.

She felt horrible about what had happened earlier. That betrayed look on Mark's face when he realized she read the letter from his sister and then didn't even tell him about it—he was so...hurt. She wished he would punish her so she could feel forgiven, but it seemed as if he was too upset to feel the least bit sexual toward her.

How would Mark react if he found out she was an undercover reporter? If she wore a wire and went through with writing a scathing exposé in the tabloid, Mark would read it and know that she had betrayed his trust.

She wanted to be worthy of Mark's trust. She wished she could work on anything but this assignment. Andrea had been so happy when she first got the job because she thought it meant that she could finally begin her career as a journalist. She thought Rodney was beginning to need her more, both professionally and personally.

She smiled sadly to herself. Rodney had proven that he wasn't any more interested in a romantic relationship with her than she was with him, and his current attitude made it pretty clear that she was skating on thin ice when it came to her career as a staff writer for the tabloid.

He didn't even want to keep her as his secretary anymore.

If Rodney fired her for refusing to write the article on Mark, her years of hard work and effort to become a journalist would have been for nothing. Word of her behavior would spread like wildfire among the major tabloids and she could count on being blacklisted, just like Rodney had threatened.

On the other hand, Mark Cannon was a good man.

Sure, he had some discrepancies between the life his PR reps presented to the public and his real life, and that could be damaging to his image. Even if people didn't care about his true history, the fact that he had allowed lies to circulate as truth would not sit well with his fans. Then there was the whole BDSM thing—which probably wouldn't fly with his more conservative fans. But Mark was a real person with real feelings and emotions, and he didn't deserve to have his privacy invaded in the ways that Rodney expected of her.

Mark deserved better than to have some woman sneak into his life and pretend to be his personal assistant. He should be able to share himself with someone who didn't have an ulterior motive such as an article to write and a career to begin.

Mark deserved better than her. He deserved a woman who could commit herself to his well-being, instead of the well-being of a stupid tabloid and a relationship with a man like Rodney.

Her priorities had been all backward, Andrea realized. She knocked on Rodney's office door firmly.

"Andrea. Glad to see you had a change of heart, babe." Rodney lifted his gelled head of hair and looking at her.

"Rodney, we have to talk."

Rodney licked his dry lips and stood, leaning his lanky body against the large oak desk. "Come here. I gotta fit you with the wire. You need to learn how to record your escapades with our hotshot movie star friend so we can have clear tapes for transcription."

"I had to sign a nondisclosure contract, Rodney, so it doesn't look like I can write the exposé after all."

"Nondisclosure my ass. What are they going to do, sue you? You're broke anyway. Now come here."

Andrea stepped toward him, feeling herself slipping back into her timid old self. Every time she spoke to Rodney she could feel her self-esteem plummet.

She shook her head resolutely. Fuck Rodney.

"Rodney. Listen to me. I'm not comfortable with wearing a wire."

"Too bad, babe. I'm the boss, or have you forgotten that too?" Rodney smirked. He took a step out from behind the desk and stood directly in front of Andrea, his arms crossed.

"I'm not okay with invading Mark Cannon's privacy for an article. It's not worth it."

Rodney laughed and picked up a folder of pictures of Mark. "Look at this guy," he said. "Mark Cannon knew what he was getting into when he decided to be an actor. Getting his privacy invaded comes with the territory."

Andrea took the folder from Rodney's grasp. She pulled out a photo of Mark walking down the street, holding a Starbucks cup in one hand.

A blush rose up from Andrea's chest as she thought of those hands stroking her face when Mark leaned down to kiss her. His strong muscular body felt like a perfect fit when she pulled him close and breathed in his masculine scent.

Just looking at Mark made her ache with longing. A tingle rushed through her body and she looked away from the photo with embarrassment. The fact that her ass was still sore from getting paddled only served to make her constantly aware of Mark's presence in her life. She could feel the heat rise in her face again.

Rodney's pale white hand grabbed the folder out of her grasp. "What's going on here?" he said. "Why did you blush when you looked at a picture of Mark Cannon?"

Andrea's eyes widened. "I don't know what you're talking about," she said lamely.

Rodney's face tightened in anger. "Something's going on here with him, isn't it? Something more than just little spanking games," Rodney snarled. "I guess I wasn't good enough for you? You think you're so high and mighty that I'm not good enough for you?" Rodney was yelling now, his face turning a frightening shade of red. A single vein bulged in his forehead.

Andrea had seen this side of her ex before, but it was usually directed at someone else. She should have known that his temper might someday be focused on her.

"Rodney, please calm down. You always said we were free to date other people, that we had no commitment to each other."

Rodney slammed his hands down on his desk. "You fucked him, didn't you, you slut?"

"You know what? This is none of your business, because we are *through*," she yelled, shocking herself with her words. She'd always thought Rodney was the best man she would ever get and that she should just put up with his patronizing and his temper and his belittling comments.

Something in Andrea had changed. She couldn't believe she felt the freedom to tell off the man who had been her boss and sometimes boyfriend for years. She didn't understand why or how, but somehow just being friends with Mark had given her the strength to stand up for herself. And feeling so cherished in his arms as she submitted to him had made her feel worthy of being desired.

Maybe she'd never end up with an incredible man like Mark, but at least she wouldn't have to settle for a loser like Rodney.

Rodney looked at her. "What are you saying, Andrea?"

Andrea pulled her shoulders back and faced Rodney's steely gaze. "I never want to hear from you again."

Rodney's mouth dropped open in shock. "What did you say to me? You know you're nothing without me, Andrea."

"Lose my number," she said softly. "If you ever get bored or lonely, don't even think of calling me."

"That's not going to work, Andrea, and you know it. I'm still your boss, and you still have an exposé to write for me about the adventures of a certain Mark Cannon."

"You're not my boss anymore, Rodney."

"Don't you walk out of here, Andrea," Rodney yelled as she turned to leave.

"I'm not writing that article for you, Rodney. I'm not going to do that to Mark. If that means that I just threw my career as a journalist away, then so be it. I quit." Andrea threw her hand up and slapped it over her mouth as if someone else had said those words.

Did she really just quit her job?

Rodney looked at her. "You can take that back, Andrea. You have ten seconds to take back what you just said, and we can pretend you never said it at all."

"No, we can't. I meant it. I don't want to work for you or for *The Hollywood Exposer* anymore. My ability to sleep at night is worth more than this job. I'm worth more."

"Oh I see," Rodney said. "You want more money. Fine. You got it. I'll raise your salary upon delivery of the article on Mark Cannon."

"No, Rodney. I'm not delivering anything at all on Mark Cannon. I don't want your money, and I don't want you."

Rodney stepped toward Andrea, his face threateningly close to hers. "You just made a huge mistake, babe. Huge. You're gonna pay for that, and so is your hotshot movie star. Everywhere you turn my photographers will be on you two like flies on shit. If you won't deliver Mark Cannon to me, then I'm just going to have to get the dirt on him myself."

"Don't do this, Rodney. You've got other scoops. Leave Mark alone."

"Just so you know, babe," Rodney said with a slow smile. "You were never cut out to be a journalist. You're too soft. I'm not going to be as gentle with Mark as you've been—I've got a tabloid to sell."

Rodney grinned at her and pulled a camera out from behind his back. The flash went off in Andrea's eyes, leaving white-hot blind spots dancing in her field of vision.

"Get used to it," Rodney said. "Have a nice trip to

New York."

* * * * *

Traffic on the 405 Freeway was lighter than usual. Andrea looked over at Mark's handsome face nervously, smoothing her hair. Why couldn't she ever have a good hair day? She had spent an hour deciding what to pack for their impromptu trip to New York.

Normally she would wear comfortable jeans for a five-hour flight cross country, but since Mark's sister would be meeting them at the airport in New York, Andrea wanted to look a bit nicer than usual. She wore a knee-length skirt, but she was probably wearing the wrong thing. Andrea glanced at Mark's casual jeans and sighed.

Her ex had often told her that she always looked out of place. Well, Rodney's opinion no longer mattered. She wouldn't have him around to make belittling comments anymore.

Mark turned toward her, his legs angling toward hers in the back of the limousine. "We should be at LAX in a few minutes. Have you ever noticed that every place in L.A. is twenty minutes away from everything else?" he asked with a smile.

Andrea laughed. "Yes Sir, unless there's traffic, and then everything takes an hour to get to."

"Even your neighbor's house."

Andrea grew warm just looking at Mark. His had a light stubble across his strong jaw and the afternoon sun filtered in through the tinted limousine windows to glow across his face. The tough denim of his jeans grazed the front of her bare knee.

They hadn't spoken of their afternoon of passion in his trailer. It was as if he had forgotten about it. She longed to move closer to him, to let his leg press against hers completely. She wondered what he would do if she slid across the seat and sat so close that they would be forced to touch.

Feeling bold, Andrea leaned forward slightly, her skirt

sliding up her leg to reveal her thigh as she pressed her knee against his. Looking at her bare thigh, she pulled her skirt down quickly. This was ridiculous. She was acting like a teenager.

Mark must have felt the sudden pressure against his knee because he looked at Andrea. He cleared his throat.

"Sorry, do you need more space?" he asked. He almost appeared as if he were embarrassed. Mark quickly scooted his whole body away from Andrea and looked out the window before she could say a word.

Andrea retreated to her side of the seat, crushed. She now knew the answer to her question of what Mark would do if she tried to sit close to him. He'd just move farther away. She hated that she wanted a man so badly, even though he found it so easy to turn off his feelings.

"Mark, about that day, in the trailer…"

"I'm over it," he said.

"Oh."

Andrea closed her eyes and listened to the sounds of traffic outside the limousine windows. They would be at the airport soon. She felt tears build up in her eyes and she willed them to go away. He was over it. Making love to him had meant everything to her and he was over it. She needed to get over it too.

Andrea heard Mark stirring around in his bag and she opened one eye out of curiosity. He took out a baseball cap and a pair of designer sunglasses.

"Sir, may I ask what're you doing?"

"We're about to go into a very public place. If we want to make it to our plane on time, I need to cover up a bit," he explained.

Andrea nodded, looking at Mark's disguise objectively. The cap covered his trademark brown hair, and the sunglasses covered just enough of his face that the average passerby would notice only a handsome man, and not immediately recognize him from the movies.

"Not that I have anything against commercial airlines,"

she said carefully, "but why didn't you want to take the producer up on his offer to borrow his private jet?"

Mark shrugged. "My family feels estranged from me as it is. I try to do what I can to not flash my money or the 'celebrity perks' I get in their faces. Little things like them picking me up from the airport in their old minivan make me feel closer to them. If I swoop onto their doorstep in a limo, talking about my private jet, it just feels weird."

"I see," Andrea said.

"I'm glad you're going with me," Mark said. "No matter what type of aircraft I'm in, I hate flying."

"Why?"

"You'll see why."

Mark watched Andrea as she scanned the long lines leading up to the security checkpoint and shook her head, as if she couldn't believe the huge numbers of people crowding through the airport.

"It's not even a holiday," she said.

"That's LAX for you," Mark said, pulling his baseball cap down lower on his forehead. So far no one had given him more than a second glance, and Mark hoped that his simple disguise would be enough for now. "Andrea, hold our place in line for a minute while I hit the men's room."

* * * * *

"Yes Sir," she replied.

Her smile was so genuine it nearly brought him to his knees every time.

Mark started off toward the men's restroom. He looked over his shoulder at Andrea, waiting patiently in line with their luggage at her feet. The line moved forward slowly and she picked up the bags and inched them up. Mark admired how gracefully she moved.

She didn't even realize how beautiful she was. A college kid stared openly at her from a few rows over. Poor guy, Mark knew how he felt. Mark's body had reacted like a teenager's when she pressed against him in the limo, her skirt pushed up her thigh. He had moved away before he could make an even bigger fool out of himself. She was going to think all he thought about was sex.

Well, there's some truth to that.

He just wished she would stop bringing up how she had hidden his sister's letter from him. He had thought it through and he was over it.

Mark shifted the backpack he had packed with little gifts for his niece, allowing the weight to distribute evenly across both shoulders. He didn't care if his checked luggage got lost, but he certainly wasn't going to arrive in New York empty-handed, even though it was a pain in the neck to hoist around a carry-on bag.

What was he thinking, really, taking this trip in the middle of his movie's production schedule? Sure, the producer had been understanding—he had even offered the use of his private jet to keep traveling time to a minimum, but Mark knew it was just because they wanted to keep their star happy. Mark also knew that it wasn't unheard of for a production company to call in the lawyers if an actor wasn't fulfilling his end of the contract.

Don't get distracted by this girl, Mark said to himself as he pushed open the door to the men's room. When the shoot was over he could date ten girls if he wanted—he just couldn't screw this up.

Mark sighed. He didn't want to date ten girls. For some reason completely unknown to him, for the first time in his life, Mark wanted to date only one girl. Andrea.

"That's crazy," Mark murmured under his breath as he finished up in front of the sink. Everyone knew he wasn't the one-woman type. Even Andrea thought he had a spare stashed away in New York. He shook his head, trying to clear his thoughts.

He walked out of the men's room and stopped when he saw his own face staring at him from the cover of a magazine at the newsstand. Flipping through it briefly, he found his thoughts turning once again to Andrea. He was definitely getting distracted by her.

By the time he got back to the security checkpoint, Andrea had moved all the way to the head of the line.

She smiled up at Mark as he stepped next to her, just in time to drop his bag onto the x-ray conveyor belt and step through the metal detector. It beeped loudly as he walked through.

A middle-aged man in a blue and white airport security uniform handed him a small gray plastic basket. "Put your sunglasses, watch and any coins or metal you may have on you in here for the x-ray machine. That should do it."

Oh no. Shit, shit, shit. He put the items in the basket, then took off his sunglasses.

"Oh wow," the guard said with a smile. "Mark Cannon. My daughter's got your posters plastered all over her bedroom."

Mark smiled and nodded. "Cool. Tell her I said hi," Mark said, stepping through the metal detector again.

Two bright flashes of light went off suddenly. Mark groaned. Paparazzi, of course. Maybe some overzealous tourists. This is why he hated flying. He heard another camera click from behind him, then another to his side.

"Hey—no photographs in the airport. Who took those pictures?" the middle-aged guard said, whirling around. No one appeared to be holding a camera.

Mark smiled tensely as he put his sunglasses and hat back on and practically pulled Andrea out of there.

CHAPTER SEVEN

"Won't it be really late in New York by the time we get in?" Andrea asked as they boarded the plane.

"With the time difference, I really thought it was going to be too late for my sister to pick us up, but she still insisted. So I insisted that if she picks us up she has to drive us straight to the hotel," Mark said.

"You know, I've never flown in first class before," Andrea said. "These seats are huge."

Mark laughed and nodded in agreement. "When I got my first lead role in a feature film, they were shooting a few scenes on location in Hawaii and they gave me a first-class plane ticket. I traded it in for a coach ticket and pocketed the difference," he said. "I was always afraid the rug would be pulled out from under me and I'd be back to square one again."

Andrea peered into his green eyes carefully. She knew all too well what it felt like to be walking on eggshells, always afraid of slipping up and having to start all over again.

"You know what, Mark?" she said quietly.

He smiled. "No, tell me."

"It's not so bad," she said simply.

Her whole life she worried about leaving what she had, what was comfortable, to try for something new. When she dated Rodney, she thought she'd never find the perfect man for her and so she might as well not even look. The idea of starting a new relationship had frightened her into immobility.

"What's not so bad?" Mark asked.

"Starting over from square one."

Mark looked at her with an intensity that made her blush. "Andrea, I've been daydreaming about tasting those lips of yours all afternoon."

Andrea took her breath in sharply, unsure if her ears were deceiving her. "I thought you were, um…over it," she said softly, her eyes wide.

"Over it?" he asked, his face inches from hers. "How could I be over the single most satisfying moment in my life?"

"But you said—"

"Oh, that. I'm over the letter, silly. God, those lips…"

"I'm yours, Sir," she whispered.

Mark's face was serious as he turned toward her in his seat, unlatching his metal seatbelt. "Not here, where everyone can see us."

Andrea looked away. "Okay."

"I just have to think of your reputation. If a group of people saw us kissing and then even one of them sold the story to the tabloids, all of the magazines and entertainment news shows would link us together. Your future boyfriends aren't going to want to think about you making out with someone else so publicly."

"My future boyfriends," Andrea repeated.

Mark frowned. "Andrea, I'm sorry. I love my job, but sometimes I wish I could be anonymous. For moments like this. So I could just grab you and kiss you now, and we could worry about whether or not it was a stupid thing to do later."

Andrea leaned back in her seat, unsure of what to do.

Why was Mark saying that he wasn't embarrassed to be seen with her in one breath, and then basically telling her outright that they would never be together in the very next breath?

Realistically, what he was saying made sense. Mark was known for his playboy ways, after all. *The Exposer* was always getting tips from people that he was out with yet another woman on his arm. If word got around that they were kissing, even if it was just a little kiss for fun, she could count on being forever thought of and referred to as a woman who briefly dated Mark Cannon.

Before he moved on to the next girl, of course.

The idea of Mark kissing another woman filled her with a disturbing feeling of jealousy and uneasiness. If she felt like this at the thought of Mark being with someone else, it made sense that a future boyfriend might feel jealous of Mark Cannon.

She didn't want to date anyone but Mark anyway—and that was not going to happen. He basically just spelled that out for her.

Mark looked at Andrea, waiting for her response.

"Sir, once the flight attendant comes out with that drink cart, the aisle will be blocked and no one will be getting up to use the toilet," she said. "I can go into the lavatory now, and then you can wait till she's past you with the drink cart and meet me."

Mark's mouth dropped open. "How'd you come up with that?"

Andrea felt heat rising up her face and she knew she must be blushing. "I don't know. I guess I thought it might be fun," she said. "You know. To join the Mile High Club." She clapped her hand over her mouth, wishing she could rewind and take back her words.

Mark leaned over and gently unlatched her seatbelt. A shiver ran down her spine as his fingers brushed against her skirt. "Get into that lavatory. I'll follow in a moment."

Andrea stood and climbed over Mark's legs into the

aisle, taking care not to look at him. She was afraid the expression on her face would give away their plan. She wanted him so badly she could feel her heart racing as she stepped into the tiny airplane lavatory.

She put the top of the toilet seat down and stood on it so that Mark would have a place to step into when he opened the door. Andrea looked around. Two people in here would be a tight fit, indeed.

What was she doing? She wasn't usually the type to do a thing like this—especially with a man like Mark Cannon. This was a man who had never made any promises of the future. He'd never given her any concrete reason to think that he was interested in being in a relationship with her. But in the heat of that moment, standing inside that tiny airplane bathroom, all Andrea could think about was how strongly her body reacted to Mark's mere presence.

She heard the little folding door creak open in front of her and Mark quickly stepped inside, locking the door. The little light brightened inside the lavatory as the lock clicked into place.

Mark wrapped his arms around Andrea's waist.

"I think you might be taller than me, standing on that thing," he whispered.

She leaned her body on his muscular frame, resting her face on his warm neck as she breathed in his cologne.

He pressed his lips to hers, kissing her deeply. She moaned softly against his lips, feeling her pulse race as he lowered his head and licked at her throat.

"You are so incredible, Andrea," he murmured. "You don't know how much you turn me on."

Mark slid one of his strong hands under her shirt. She shivered as his smooth, cool hand ran up her back.

"Oh Mark," she whispered, resting her head against the wall and pushing herself back. The muscles in her back pressed against his hand and relaxed as he kneaded them slowly.

Mark looked at her face as she wrapped her arms

around his neck, pulling him toward her.

"I wish I had made you wear a butt plug before we got on this flight, so I would know it was in you, even when we're just sitting there talking," he whispered, nibbling at her lower lip. He plunged his tongue into her mouth, restraining her from responding.

She accepted his kiss, grateful not to have to tell him what was on her mind.

She didn't want to tell him that she still had layers of guilt and confusion when it came to relationships. Andrea kissed Mark hungrily, feeling the pressure from his body pushing against her leg.

"You're so beautiful, Andrea..."

Beautiful. How she wanted to believe him. She knew she wasn't, she couldn't be... Mark slid his hands out from under her blouse and rubbed them up her arms and across her shoulders. He held both of her hands in his and gently lifted them above her head. He leaned Andrea back against the wall and nibbled her earlobe.

"That tickles," she whispered.

"I can do so many things to you that will tickle," he breathed into her ear.

Andrea's eyes widened at the thought.

"You're so beautiful when you do that," he said, brushing his lips with hers.

Can't be true, but nice to hear, she thought, turning her head to hide her blush.

Mark looked at her. "Come on, don't keep ignoring me. I want you to acknowledge that I think you're beautiful." He leaned in and teased her trembling lip with little nipping kisses.

"But, Sir... I know I'm not beautiful," she whispered. She didn't want anyone to hear them and realize that two people were in the bathroom.

Mark raised her arms higher above her head, resting her hands against the wall with gentle pressure from one of his hands. He let his other hand slide underneath her knee-length skirt, caressing her thigh.

"Andrea," he said sweetly, "you're not going anywhere until you respond the way I want."

Her heartbeat quickened as Mark slowly tickled up her bare leg and flicked her clit. She gasped.

"Mmm," he said. "That's a nice response, but not the one I'm looking for."

She breathed in deeply as he parted her lips with his wet tongue. "You're beautiful, Andrea. So…amazingly…beautiful."

Andrea tried to pull her hands away from Mark's grasp so that she could hide her face from his staring green eyes. He resisted and held her hands firmly in place as he built up a rhythm, flicking her clit over and over until she was so close to coming that she was stifling her moans.

"Please, Sir, I'm going to come," she gasped, fighting the sensation until he gave his permission.

He changed the position of his hand, interrupting the rhythm on her clit and deftly inserted three fingers into her pussy.

"Mark," she cried softly as he made a "come hither" motion with his fingers inside her pussy. He hit directly against her G-spot while thumbing her clit slowly. "Please—"

"Come," he said, and she let the sensation overwhelm her as she came hard, bucking against his fingers.

"Thank you," she whispered. He thought she was beautiful and, at least for now, she would let herself believe that it was true. Tears welled in her eyes as she hugged him close, kissing his mouth.

Then the little seatbelt warning sign flickered on above the sink with a pert *ding*.

"We should get back to our seats, Sir," Andrea said.

"We'll go when I say we're done." Mark wrapped his arms around her waist and smoothly switched their positions in the cramped bathroom so that he sat on the closed toilet seat and she stood in front of him. He pressed his hands down on her shoulders and she dropped to her knees in front of him.

The seatbelt warning sign *dinged* again. Andrea looked at him, concerned, as the plane rocked with turbulence. "Sir?"

"You better suck my cock quick, honey, if you want to get back to your seat."

Andrea unzipped his jeans and his huge cock practically sprang out in her hand. She didn't hesitate, taking his entire length into her mouth even as she gagged at the unfamiliar sensation.

"Swallow my cock," he said, inhaling sharply as she did just that. He wrapped her hair in his fist until he had complete control of her head. Andrea breathed through her nose as he slid her mouth back and forth over his cock. With a final thrust, he came hard, spurting a hot jet of salty cum down the back of her throat.

"Thank me," he prompted.

"Thank you, Sir." She smiled up at him, accepting his hand to help her stand.

"I'll meet you back at our seats," Mark said, giving her one final kiss before he straightened them both out, washed his hands and flushed the commode. He carefully opened the door for her.

A flash popped in their faces as soon as Mark opened the door. Andrea gasped as the photographer's camera clicked over and over again.

"Hey—what do you think you're doing?" Mark growled at the photographer. Andrea blinked, white spots dancing in front of her eyes from the flash.

"Mark Cannon—surely you can do better than her," the photographer said, taking another picture.

No way. Rodney?

"Paparazzi," Mark yelled, slamming the camera down so that it hung by its strap around the photographer's neck, revealing a pale face.

"Rodney!" Andrea couldn't believe that Rodney had

followed them with his camera.

Mark looked at Rodney's face in confusion. "Aren't you Andrea's boyfriend? Didn't you visit the movie set?"

"Ex-boyfriend!" Andrea shouted.

Rodney laughed, throwing his gelled head back. "Ex-boyfriend, it seems." Mark grabbed for the camera but Rodney pulled back quickly. "Watch it, Mark Cannon, or you're gonna have a messy lawsuit on your hands."

Andrea stepped out of the lavatory, her hair in tangles, her lip gloss completely licked off by Mark's kisses. "Rodney, you jerk."

"Looks like you've been keeping busy, babe," Rodney said with a sneer. He leaned in and whispered in Andrea's ear, dropping his voice so Mark wouldn't be able to hear him. "Don't worry. I won't tell Mark who you really are, 'cause I have a feeling you're gonna smarten up and decide to work for me again."

"Never," Andrea said, pulling away from Rodney's smoky breath.

Mark grabbed Rodney and pulled him away from Andrea. "Leave her alone, Rodney."

A flight attendant appeared in the aisle behind Rodney. "Sir, ma'am, please take your seats. The captain has turned on the fasten seatbelt sign."

Rodney looked over his shoulder at the flight attendant. "Shut up," he said.

The flight attendant narrowed her eyes. "Sir, do not tell me to shut up. Either take your seat now or you will be arrested upon our arrival in New York."

Rodney grinned and backed slowly down the narrow aisle. "Chill, babe. I'll sit down." He looked at Mark. "I got what I wanted, anyway." Rodney turned and walked to the back of the plane.

The flight attendant closed the blue curtain that separated the aisle between the first-class seats and the coach seats. "I'm so sorry about that, Mr. Cannon. We're so pleased that you chose to fly with us, and we do hope you'll choose our airline again for all your travel needs. If you could please take a seat as the captain has turned on the fasten seatbelt sign. We may experience some turbulence."

Mark looked at Andrea in confusion as they sat and latched the metal seatbelts. "What on earth is Rodney doing here?" he asked. "Why is he taking our picture?"

Andrea glanced around the first-class cabin, grateful that Rodney was seated in coach. "Rodney is trying to make me regret leaving him."

It was true, after all. Of course, the fact that Rodney was trying to make her regret leaving him as an employee for *The Hollywood Exposer* was best left unsaid.

"He took our picture, Andrea. Hooking up in the airplane lavatory like a couple of horny college kids. What's he going to do with that?" Mark asked.

"I'm guessing we'll see it published as an exclusive on the front page of *The Hollywood Exposer* by tomorrow morning," she said grimly.

"Oh, man. Not now. Not when I'm about to visit my family for the first time in over a year," Mark groaned.

"I'm sorry, Mark. This is all my fault," Andrea said. "I told him we were going to New York before I broke it off permanently with him."

"Why the paparazzi act? Why is he taking our picture, for goodness sake?" Mark's face was a mask of anger and hurt.

"Tabloids buy photos of celebrities, the juicier the better," she said. "You know that."

"I hate those stupid supermarket tabloids," Mark said furiously.

"Me too, Sir."

She really did, she realized. She had let herself get wrapped up in what she thought was a blossoming journalistic career, but it was all just garbage. It hurt people.

When she first asked for a chance to write an article for

Rodney, she had never thought of movie stars as real people. But Mark was a real person, a man who cared about whether or not his name got run down into the ground.

She would never work for another tabloid, and certainly not for Rodney. She didn't care how much money he threw at her.

Andrea sighed. If only she could tell Mark the truth, but what could she say? *Sir, I've been meaning to tell you that I was actually working as an undercover reporter, but that's all over with.*

Andrea imagined Mark throwing her out of his life in hurt and anger. She wished she could tell him how much he had changed her, and how she'd never go back to the way she was.

Sorry, Mark, I've betrayed you in the past, but I'll never do it again.

No matter how she said it, he would hate her. But still...she had to tell him the truth—even if it meant he never wanted to see her again.

CHAPTER EIGHT

As they walked through JFK airport, Andrea felt as though a weight had been lifted from her shoulders. Telling Mark the truth about the tabloid wouldn't be easy, but as soon as they had a moment alone at the hotel she would sit him down and explain everything. He deserved to know.

Mark nodded toward the sign pointing the way to the baggage claim area. "My sister said she'd be waiting out front of the baggage claim area, but security never lets the cars stay put for more than a moment or so, so she's probably circling around right now."

"I'd like to go the ladies' room before we leave if that's okay—may I meet you at the baggage carousel?" Andrea said.

Mark grinned at Andrea, his straight white teeth seeming even whiter under the fluorescent glow of the harsh airport lights. "You may," he said with a wink.

She looked back over her shoulder at him as she walked away. He was watching her and smiling. She couldn't help but smile back.

Then Rodney walked around the corner and grabbed Andrea's arm.

She had felt Rodney's presence before she even saw

him. A shiver of disgust ran down her spine and she turned to face her ex-boyfriend angrily. "What do you want, Rodney? Enough is enough."

Rodney threw his arm around her shoulders and pulled her close to him.

Andrea looked back toward Mark. He was already running toward them, his green eyes blazing.

Rodney squeezed her arm. "Get rid of him or he's dead meat. I mean it. Dead meat," Rodney whispered.

Andrea stared at Rodney in horror. Was he really that crazy? He had followed them to New York, for crying out loud. And now he seemed…off. Something wasn't right. Yes, he just might be that crazy.

Mark glared at Rodney, his broad chest heaving with exertion. "Get away from her. She doesn't want to talk to you," Mark said.

"That's not true, is it, Andrea?" Rodney said. "Because if you don't want to talk to me in private, then I'll just have to do all the talking with Mark right here, and I don't think you want that."

Rodney's breath smelled as though he had indulged in a couple of in-flight cocktails after their confrontation on the plane.

"What's he talking about?" Mark asked Andrea.

Andrea looked at Mark's confused expression. She knew if Rodney told Mark that she had been working for the tabloid as an undercover reporter, he would never trust her again.

She needed to be the one to tell him, in a quiet moment, in private, in a way that gave her at least some opportunity to try to explain herself. If Rodney blew her cover, he would do it as cruelly as possible. Mark would get hurt.

Andrea looked around frantically. She saw at least two of Rodney's thugs in the crowd. Forget hurt feelings, Mark could actually get physically hurt. She needed to get him out of there.

Andrea sighed. "Mark, I'm so sorry. I need you to trust that I have a reason for talking to Rodney right now. Please, Sir, let me just take care of this."

Mark looked at her with a hurt expression. "You can't seriously want to be left alone with this jerk," he said. "Come on. My sister is waiting outside."

"Don't worry about me, Sir. I'll take care of this. He just wants to apologize for his behavior—I just need a moment alone, that's all. You go on ahead and don't worry, okay?" She looked at Mark and forced herself to smile.

Mark didn't return the smile. "I'm not comfortable leaving you here with your psycho ex-boyfriend. Come with me."

Rodney's arm tensed against her back. "Dead meat," he whispered in a tone so low that Andrea knew that it was meant for her ears only. Outwardly, he grinned at Andrea and Mark. "I won't keep her long," Rodney said to Mark.

Andrea closed her eyes. *Please let Mark understand that this is for his own good. Please don't let him be hurt.*

"Mark, I don't mean any disrespect," she said carefully, knowing she was about as far from being a submissive assistant at that moment as she could be. "I know you want me to listen to you, but I can explain my behavior in just a few minutes. Please, Sir."

Mark threw his hands up in frustration. "Fine. Whatever. Talk to the drunk ex who's stalking you. I'll have my sister pull into the parking garage across the street, so meet us there. First floor."

Mark turned stiffly and walked away, his jaw clenched. Andrea watched with increasing agitation as Mark pulled his baseball cap lower over his forehead and cursed under his breath.

He turned back and said, "If you're not there in fifteen minutes, I'm coming back in to look for you. I don't trust this guy as far as I can throw him."

Rodney relaxed his grip on Andrea as Mark walked

SHOSHANNA EVERS

farther and farther away, until Andrea couldn't distinguish him amongst the hundreds of other men in the crowded airport.

"He's gone," she said, pulling her arm away from Rodney. "You happy?"

"Not happy yet," he said. "We need to talk. You and me." His face got a little too close to hers and she pulled away even more.

"There's really nothing to talk about, Rodney," Andrea said, her voice low and steady. "I'm through with you and I'm through with the tabloid. You've got your stupid pictures—so go. Go have fun and leave us alone."

"I want you," Rodney said.

Andrea winced at the sickly sweet smell on his breath. "Too bad, you're not my boyfriend anymore."

"Don't flatter yourself. I never was your boyfriend," Rodney snarled. "And I don't want you that way. Who would?"

Andrea felt tears of humiliation blur her vision. She hated how Rodney's cruel words stung. She couldn't let him get to her—she deserved better.

Rodney looked at her tears and smiled. "I want you to work for me again. I want the full scoop, and I want it now."

"Don't be crazy, Rodney. You've got plenty. You don't need me anymore."

"I've got some photos, I could make up some lies, but you've obviously been doing a lot more than just helping your little movie star answer his fan mail," he said, licking his dry lips. "You're his lover."

"That is none of your business. Besides, what you saw on that plane is not indicative of our relationship."

"I want those details. What's he like behind closed bedroom doors, everything. The things he does to you, the things he makes you do. I want private pictures. Full frontal. I'll make a fortune. Just think of how much the public will pay to get juicy details like that." Rodney was practically salivating at the thought.

"First of all, you are sick in the head. Second, I'm not working for you. In any capacity. Ever."

"This isn't over. Don't think for a second that this is over." He squeezed her shoulder hard enough to make her wince and then, just as suddenly, leaned in and gave her a kiss on the cheek. Andrea started to protest but Rodney took a step back and waved her off as if she were an annoying fly he was trying to shoo away. "Go on now. Mark's waiting for his faithful assistant."

* * * * *

Walking out of the automatic glass doors toward the parking garage, Andrea's legs felt wobbly. Rodney was such a creep—and it seemed as if he would never let her out of his grasp. It was horrible.

Now she'd have to put on a smile for Mark's sister and pretend that all Rodney had wanted to do was apologize for his atrocious behavior in-flight. Andrea stopped and took a deep breath to calm herself—she was pretty sure she looked rumpled after the long flight.

Mark must have stepped out of his sister's car when he saw her walking toward them because he was leaning against the hood, a concerned look marring his handsome face.

"Are you okay?" he asked. "What did that creep want?"

"I'm fine, Sir." She smiled thinly.

"You don't look fine. What did he say to you?"

"He was just…being Rodney. I made my feelings very clear. Please, let's just go and not let him ruin your visit."

"We can talk about it later at the hotel—not in front of my sister."

"Where are we going to be staying?"

"Well, we're in New York City," Mark said, "so I think we should go to the Ritz."

"I've heard of it. I've also heard that the cost of staying there for one night is more than my rent in L.A. for a whole month."

"Don't worry about that. If you can't afford your own room you are more than welcome to stay in mine." Mark put his arm around her shoulder and suddenly her anger over the whole Rodney situation melted away.

Andrea laughed. "Sneaky, Sir. It looks like you've got yourself a roommate for the night."

"You'll love it. We'll have a view of Central Park. Besides, did you really think I'd let you stay all by yourself in the big bad city?"

"Something tells me I'd be safer on my own, Sir."

"Yeah, you would," he said, smiling. "I'm going to ravage you."

Mark's sister Katherine came out of the car while they were talking and smiled, extending her hand. Katherine looked exactly like Mark.

"You must be Andrea. I've heard so much about you."

Andrea raised her eyebrows and looked at Mark, who shrugged. Mark had been talking about her to his family? *Interesting.* "Thank you. It's so nice to finally meet you."

Katherine smiled and gestured toward the car. "I wish you'd reconsider and just stay at our apartment, Mark. I hate to drive family to some impersonal hotel."

"I appreciate the thought, Kath—but Mom's probably already asleep, and so is everyone else. We'll just show up in the morning bright and early for breakfast, okay?"

Andrea sat in the backseat behind Mark. She kept looking at the little hairs on the back of his neck—they seemed to shine like tiny wisps of wheat whenever headlights shone through the window.

Katherine chattered on amiably about how happy she was to see Mark and to finally meet one of Mark's friends. "He never brings dates home, you know," she said.

Andrea sputtered. "I'm—I'm—"

Mark interrupted. "You're what? Not my date?"

Andrea stared, unsure what he wanted her to say. "What do you mean?"

Mark laughed. "Well, we're on a vacation together. If

that's not a date, then it's at least very close to being something like that, right?"

Andrea grinned back at him. "I guess so. If you say so." She was so giddy at the thought of them officially dating that for a moment she almost forgot that he still didn't know the truth about her—and that would change everything.

Katherine nodded her head in agreement as she drove through the city. "Of course you are. Even if it is a new relationship."

Andrea smoothed her skirt and looked out the window at all the city lights.

"Here we are," Katherine said as she pulled to a stop in front of the Ritz. "Okay, I've got to drop this car off back at my friend Shelly's lot. She lent me the car."

"What?" Mark asked. "What happened to your minivan?"

"We sold it," Katherine said. "It just didn't make sense to pay for a parking garage here in New York City when we could just take the subway everywhere and cabs when needed."

"I'll buy you a car. And a parking space," Mark said.

Katherine shook her head. "We've talked about that, Mark. Tom would never agree to a handout like that. We're doing fine. Thank you, though."

Andrea watched this exchange silently. It was nice of Mark to offer his sister money, but it was even nicer that she wasn't mooching off him. Like Andrea was. She never should have accepted his offer to pay for her first-class plane ticket. Then again, he had said he wanted to and that he wanted her to sit with him, and that meant first class. And of course he was paying for the hotel now as well...

"Okay, out, out," Katherine said. "I'm about to fall asleep at the wheel."

"Thanks for the lift, Katherine. We'll see you tomorrow, right?" Andrea asked as she slid out of the car.

"Bright and early," Katherine said as Mark grabbed

their suitcases out of the trunk.

Andrea waited for Katherine to drive off before she put her hand on Mark's shoulder.

"You ready to go in?" he asked, lifting her suitcase.

Andrea shook her head, and to her horror, tears came to her eyes. "We need to talk."

She felt as if she had been kicked in the stomach. Or the head. She felt as if she was going to vomit and pass out at the same time. This was it—he had to know.

He had a right to know the truth. She had already decided that telling him would be the best thing to do. It was the only right thing to do. So why was her mouth so dry? Why did the words die in her throat?

"Andrea? Are you okay?"

She licked her dry lips and smiled.

Mark set the suitcase back down and looked at her. "Wait a minute. Is this about that whole dating thing? Because this doesn't have to be like a date if you're not comfortable with that. You could just be my assistant. Well, my special sort of assistant."

"No," Andrea said. "It's not that at all. It's actually about being your assistant."

Mark watched her, saying nothing.

"I, um, I used to work as a secretary for Rodney."

"Wait a minute," Mark interrupted. "What do you mean, you worked for Rodney?"

"Rodney was my supervisor and we also kind of dated," she explained.

Mark became very still. "I thought you said you actually didn't have experience as a submissive—so do you just fuck every guy you work for? You hooked up with Rodney, you hooked up with me. Any others?"

"Please, Mark, it wasn't like that. And no, no others. But I broke up with Rodney. And I quit my job."

Mark laughed, relief washing over his face. "Is that all?"

Andrea took a deep breath and exhaled slowly. "Mark, I was a secretary at *The Hollywood Exposer*. That's why

Rodney's been stalking you."

The laughter in Mark's voice was gone. "He's going to publish that picture of us."

"Most likely, yes."

"I can't believe this," he said.

Andrea sighed and looked down at her hands, which were trembling. She had to tell him everything. Now. "I was offered a chance to write a feature story on you. I...declined."

Mark's face went strangely blank. "When were you planning on telling me this?"

"I'm so sorry. I quit my job there. It's over, Sir." Andrea swiped at a rogue tear that she could feel trailing down her cheek. "I couldn't sell you out, Mark. Not after getting to know you."

"So you thought about selling me out before then?"

"I didn't know you then, and being a journalist has always been my dream. I'm so sorry, Sir." She turned her back, hiding her face in her hands. "I understand if you never want to see me again—"

Her words were cut off abruptly as Mark spun her around and kissed her hard on the mouth. "Shut up," he said, kissing her again.

Andrea looked up at his green eyes warily. "Do you want me to leave?"

Mark shook his head and kissed her, softer this time. "I said shut up. If you're done with that horrible tabloid then it's a non-issue. You're not a secretary anymore. You're my personal assistant."

Andrea nearly wept with relief as she threaded her hands through his thick brown hair. "Your very personal assistant."

"Yeah you are." He shouldered his luggage and picked up her suitcase with one hand, taking her hand in his with the other. "I'm nervous about seeing my family again tomorrow after all this time. Dumb, right? But I'm glad you're here with me. Tell me you're done with Rodney."

Andrea nodded, her heart pounding in her chest as she waited for the other shoe to drop. "Yes Sir."

"Say it."

"I'm done with Rodney, Sir. I'm…yours."

"And you're done with the tabloid?"

"Yes Sir. Forever and ever. I'm done."

"You didn't actually do anything, then, right? You didn't write the article. You didn't sell me out."

Andrea felt the guilt that had burdened her for weeks lift away as she realized that what Mark had said was true. "No, I didn't sell you out, Mark. I never will."

"So let's just forget this whole thing for now. Tonight I'm going to whip you for it, though."

Andrea nodded. She couldn't believe how well he had taken her confession. Wait a minute, a whipping?

"Let's get off this sidewalk and get into bed," he suggested.

"Yeah, I'm beat."

Mark grinned mischievously. "I wasn't planning on letting you sleep. You still have your punishment coming to you."

CHAPTER NINE

"Wow—I can't believe we could just get a room in the middle of the night," Andrea said as they took the elevator up to their suite. Mark grinned at her—she was cute without even trying.

"That's one of the perks of New York. You know what's another perk?"

Andrea shook her head, touching his hand.

Mark looked at her and smoothed a piece of long dark hair out of her eyes. "Having you all to myself."

Andrea smiled at him and he felt his heart hammer in his chest. Man—was he falling for her? He was really starting to care about her—and that was a scary thought. He'd never let anyone into his life before like he had with Andrea. He'd definitely never taken a girl home to meet the family, that's for sure.

The fact that she turned down an opportunity to sell him out to the tabloids only proved how much he could trust her, especially since she had dreamed of being a journalist. He touched her fingertips lightly as they stood side by side in the elevator.

Tonight, she was all his.

* * * * *

Andrea pressed her fingertips against the cool glass as she stood by the window overlooking Central Park. She fingered the brocade drapes. They must be expensive. The whole suite looked expensive—the richly patterned rugs, the gleaming wood of the table and the deep plush of the sofas. But the best thing was this view.

Mark stepped out of the marble bathroom wearing only the hotel bathrobe, his brown hair still wet from his shower. Hmmm, maybe this was a better view, actually. He walked across the room and stood in front of her.

"You are wearing way too much clothing," he murmured as he started unbuttoning her blouse. She moved to help him but he brushed her fingers away. "Don't help. Stay perfectly still. I've been fantasizing about getting you naked since we got off the plane."

Andrea forced her breathing to slow down as he deftly opened her blouse to her navel and let it fall off her shoulders. He unsnapped her bra with one hand as he let his thumb slide under the front, grazing her nipple. She arched her back to allow him more access and he laughed.

"Impatient, huh?" He caressed her nipples, pushing her bra to the floor. "Better relax, honey. This is going to take forever."

"Forever sounds good," she said, her breath catching as he brought his mouth down over her nipple.

She felt his warm hand slide over her back, kneading her muscles as his tongue played over her breasts, creating a line of passion that seemed directly connected to the need she was feeling in her pussy. She reached out to open his robe and he held her wrist in his hand, restraining her.

"I'm not done with you," he said.

He unzipped the top of her skirt and pushed it down her thighs, where it joined her other clothing on the deep carpet. He let her wrist go only to capture her hips with his hands, letting his fingers slide under the strings of the only scrap of clothing she had left. With one quick movement he ripped them off her.

Andrea gasped. "Sir—that was my only nice pair of panties."

"Let me make it up to you." He touched her, slowly, finding her clit, creating a rhythm that she thought would make her faint. Her knees went weak and he lifted her up in his arms and carried her to the bed before she could even find the words to protest. Not that she would. This was heaven on earth.

Mark kissed her, his mouth covering hers with a ferocity that she'd never felt before. She felt so wanted and desired. She opened his robe and slid her hand down his chest, loving the feel of his muscles flexing as he continued touching her, rubbing her clit, dipping his fingers into her slick pussy.

"Please, Sir," she said. "Fuck me."

Mark breathed deeply and nodded. "I've never wanted anybody as much as I want you," he said as he climbed out of the bed and crossed the suite. "And that freaks me the hell out."

"Sir?"

He didn't respond, just rummaged through his luggage until he turned back to her with a smile, brandishing a short, thin whip.

"Turn over and hold on to the bedpost," he ordered.

Andrea's stomach fluttered but she did as he said, reaching above her head to brace herself against one of the tall mahogany bedposts. The first lash on her ass cheeks made her cry out. It hurt, but in a good way—a feeling that she never had experienced before she met Mark.

"I'm going to have to gag you so I don't have to worry about security breaking down the door," he said. "I'll judge when your whipping is done by the red marks on your skin. When I decide you are appropriately marked, I'll stop—but not a moment sooner. Do I have your consent?"

Andrea nodded, both terrified and completely aroused. "What if it's too much, Sir?" she asked.

"It will be," he said, popping her ripped panties in her mouth. Her tongue was pushed flat and she could smell her own arousal on the material as she forced herself to breathe calmly through her nose.

She held on again, crying out against the gag as he whipped her ass and thighs, the lashes alternating between light caresses and sharp strokes that had her body pressing against the bedpost to get away. Suddenly he stopped and she felt his tongue gently licking one long stroke from her ass cheek up to her mid back.

"That was beautiful, Andrea," he said. "You have such a beautiful ass. I have to fuck you in this gorgeous ass of yours."

Andrea shook her head no without meaning to—it was just that she'd never had anyone touch her back there.

"I'm not giving you a chance to say no to this, Andrea. I've been very lenient with you, since I'm really only particularly dominant in the bedroom, and I'm not too interested in having a slave the rest of the time. But make no mistake about it, Andrea," he said, holding her chin in his hands, staring into her eyes, "I am the boss right now. What I say goes, and if you have a problem with that you are welcome to leave. But we'll be done—because as much as I...like you, I can't be with a woman who won't submit to me in bed."

He pulled the panties out of her mouth. "Speak."

"I want to submit to you in bed," she said truthfully. "I'm just scared, Sir."

"I'll make it very easy for you, then. I'm going to tie you up and gag you so you have absolutely no need to fight what we both know you truly want. Are we agreed?"

"Yes Sir."

"I have your consent to tie you up, gag you and do whatever I want to you?"

Andrea swallowed and nodded. Why was she so afraid? She did want this. She wanted him. "Yes Sir, I'm yours completely."

Mark smiled and kissed her lips softly. "Good girl. Now bend over the bed."

Andrea did what he said, her ass and thighs burning from the whipping he had just given her. Mark took the sash from his robe and tied it securely around her wrists and then tied that to one of the bedposts. Once her hands were tied, she heard him go back to his luggage. She tried to see what he was doing but she couldn't twist the right way. She could feel it, though, as he took one of his silk cords and tied it around her ankle, securing it to another bedpost. When he tied her other ankle to the opposite bedpost, she was bent over and splayed open for him.

Curious, she tried to free herself from her bonds. She couldn't move more than an inch and she couldn't close her legs at all.

"As much as I loved you having your soaked panties in your mouth, I'm going to gag you with something that I can control a bit better," he murmured. She felt some sort of sash being tied between her lips and then around the back of her head.

His fingers reached into her pussy. She knew she was dripping wet.

"Good," he said.

Something cold and slippery dripped down her ass crack, and she gasped against the gag. He was really going to do this. But only one slim finger slid into her ass, caressing her, spreading the lube deep within her. She relaxed against his hand, loving the feeling of him opening her up for him. Then two fingers had her panting and moaning, desperate for more.

He pressed the head of his latex-sheathed cock against her asshole and despite her desire she tried to move her body forward, away from the invasion—but she couldn't. Her legs tried to close of their own accord, even though she wanted this desperately—at least in her mind. The actual experience was erotically painful. Her legs could not close.

"Just relax," he whispered. "There's nowhere to go, nothing to do but just accept it. Breathe in and relax."

She tried to take his advice as his cock filled her, stretching her asshole until she moaned, grateful for the gag and the bonds that kept her still. Soon he began thrusting, gently at first, until he reached around and felt how very wet she had become. Then he fucked her harder.

He pulled out and drove his cock inside her as deep as he could, keeping his fingers on her clit, playing with it, even pinching it soundly with each thrust. She came so hard she nearly fainted.

* * * * *

The next morning, after an early shower together, Andrea thumbed through some sightseeing brochures as she waited for Mark to finish brushing his teeth. Mark certainly looked really good wet. No wonder his beach film had been such a hit.

"I was thinking about taking one of those red double-decker tour buses around New York today," Andrea called to him, raising her voice enough to carry through the closed door. "It'll give you and your family a chance to have some private family time—and I'll get to see the sights."

"You don't have to do that," Mark said, coming out of the bathroom.

"I want to, Sir. It'll be fun. Besides, this way your family can have you all to themselves. I've heard the tours are amazing—you can get on and off the bus at different sights, or stay on and hear the whole tour."

"Now you're making *me* want to go on the tour," he joked.

"Maybe we can meet up later tonight for dinner?" she suggested. "As much as I want to get to know your family, you guys have a lot of catching up to do, Sir."

Mark nodded. "You're right. We can meet at my sister's house for dinner, and then you and I will come back to the hotel for the night."

He looked at Andrea and a shiver of anticipation ran down her spine.

"I'm looking forward to it," she said.

* * * * *

Andrea was glad she'd brought her camera. It seemed as if every sight on the tour was better than the last, and she had the perfect view from the open-air upper deck of the red bus tour. Buildings and streets and areas that she'd only ever read about or seen in movies were suddenly right there, close enough to touch. She'd spent all morning on the downtown loop, and had seen the Empire State Building, Greenwich Village, SoHo, Little Italy, Chinatown, Times Square, and Rockefeller Center.

She only hopped off a few times—there was no way she could go to New York City and not go to the top of the Empire State Building for a photo—and she got out and walked around a bit in Times Square, which was so busy and hectic and bright she almost felt overwhelmed. Almost. The city had a vibrant undercurrent that even Los Angeles couldn't replicate. There were just so many people.

The next stop was St. Patrick's Cathedral. Andrea leaned over the side of the upper deck to admire it, debating whether or not to get off the bus to see the inside, when she saw Rodney get on the very tour bus she was on.

No!

She started toward the stairway that led to the lower tier of the bus but was thwarted by the throng of tourists anxious to get off to see the Cathedral for themselves. Defeated, she sat and tried to become invisible, but it was no use. Rodney came up to the upper deck and sat next to her, effectively trapping her in her seat.

"What the hell?" Andrea said to him. She was determined to keep her cool but she could feel her palms get sweaty. "Why are you stalking me?"

"Get real. I'm not stalking you, babe. I'm stalking Mark

Cannon."

"Oh, that's so much better," she said sarcastically. "I guess you figured wherever I go, he'll go?"

"That's about the gist of it, yeah."

"Well, you've wasted your time." She pointed to his tour bus ticket and shook her head. "And you wasted your money. Mark's not here. It's just me."

"You should try the Uptown loop next time, babe. You'll get to see Broadway and Central Park."

Andrea bit her tongue before she could say that she'd already seen Central Park. No need to give him any more information. "Thanks for the tip. Now get the hell off this bus."

"Come back to work for me. You know you want to. Mark Cannon is just using you. He's going to leave you—and you'll have nothing. You'll have no Mark and no job."

"I told you before and I will tell you again. I. Will. Never. Work. For. You. *Ever.*" Her voice rose in a crescendo and to her embarrassment, tears came to her eyes in her anger and frustration.

"You're sure of that?" Rodney asked, pulling out his cell phone.

"I'm sure of it."

"Then I have no use for you as an undercover reporter. Hope you don't mind if I blow your cover." Rodney smiled as his long skinny fingers jabbed at the buttons on his cell phone.

Andrea smiled. "No need. I already blew my own cover. Yesterday. So you're too late, cretin."

Rodney's face paled. But then he laughed in her face. "Did you happen to show him this week's edition of *The Exposer*?"

Andrea didn't answer. Something was up, she could see it in his eyes.

"I'll take that as a no," he said. "It was so ambitious of you to come to my office and feed me stories about one Mr. Mark Cannon. You gave me so much dirt that I was able to write a full cover story about it."

Andrea shook her head in confusion. "I never—"

"Yes. You did. And I paid you for your betrayal of your precious movie star."

"No, no that never—"

"The check's in the mail. Thank you for being such a good inside source. I hope you don't mind that I named you as my source in the article."

Andrea felt faint. What had she told him? Nothing on purpose, of course, but Mark wouldn't know that. He'd just see the article and think she sold him out.

"I think Mark Cannon has a right to know how his little personal assistant betrayed him, don't you?"

Rodney held his cell phone like a weapon. And it was a weapon—one that would destroy her relationship with Mark forever.

"Rodney—no. Don't do it, I need to tell him myself," Andrea cried, throwing herself at his arm. He raised his cell phone away from her grasp and spoke into it. "Our friend Mark Cannon is at his sister's. Go find him and tell him who Andrea Landley really is."

Andrea's mouth dropped open in shock. Mark would never talk to her again. She'd never even get a chance to see him and explain the whole story. She should never have told Rodney they were going to New York. Or that he hadn't seen his family in a long time. Oh no...even with just that bit that she remembered telling him, Rodney could spin a very personal story about Mark.

Rodney laughed at Andrea's dazed expression. "And don't you worry, my men have documents and paystubs to prove that you were working for *The Hollywood Exposer* as a paid source. We'll even get some photos of Mark's face as he realizes that he's been betrayed so completely by his little Andrea."

"You bastard," she whispered. "How do you sleep at night?"

"I sleep like a baby, babe," Rodney said as he climbed

down the bus stairs. Andrea leaned over the upper rail, watching as he laughed and got off the tour bus just as it pulled away from the curb, taking her to the next city hot spot—and even farther away from Mark's sister's apartment.

She had to get to Mark before Rodney's men did.

She fumbled through her purse until she grasped her cell phone. She found Mark's number and hit send, feeling her heart race as she listened to the line ring.

"Hi, leave a message and I'll get back to you." *Beep.* Andrea hung up, unable to bring herself to leave her confession on his voicemail. She remembered how Mark had told her that only a few people in the world had his cell phone number—his mother, his agent at William Morris, Steven Spielberg and her.

She dialed again. *Pick up, Mark. Pick up.* Voicemail again. "Um, Mark," she said into his machine. "I—uh, I need to talk to you. I need to explain something to you, please, please call me back. I'm on my way back to your sister's—" *Beep.* His voicemail had cut her off mid-sentence.

Andrea dropped her face into her hands. She needed to get to him before they did. Her relationship with Mark depended on it.

She texted him. *Sir, call me ASAP.*

She walked down from the upper deck of the bus, right past the tour guide talking. On the lower level, she went toward the bus door and nearly wailed in frustration at the crush of people in her way.

Andrea knew that Mark needed to learn that she had met him under false pretenses. That was before she knew the real man behind the movie star image. When she thought of him as a subject to tear down in a tabloid article. Who knew where Rodney's people were hanging out? They could be staked out in the diner across the street from Mark's sister's house for all she knew.

The fact that she was on a bus headed the wrong

way—and they weren't—meant that they would get to Mark before she did. She was well aware of what they would do. They'd sit him down and tell him that she had betrayed him and that she couldn't be trusted. They'd produce papers and documents to back up their words. They'd make him feel like the stupidest man alive for ever having trusted her.

But she needed Mark to trust her, from the bottom of her soul. He had changed her. Andrea would never be the same again now that she had known his powerful kiss and intense green eyes.

She was in love with him. She loved Mark Cannon.

The thought stopped Andrea cold. She inhaled sharply, breathing in the scent of dozens of tourists packed together.

She had probably said those very words before, but it was in a childish, starstruck fan sort of way. She had heard teenage girls gushing over his movie posters, going on about how they loved Mark Cannon, how he was so hot and they just loved him. This was different. Very, very different.

Andrea loved Mark Cannon in a way she had thought was reserved strictly for fairy tales and Hollywood movies. In a forever kind of way. She longed for Mark and, for all she knew, she would never see him again.

She had never allowed herself to fall in love before, fearing she wouldn't be loved in return. She'd always had her armor on, but somehow Mark Cannon had pierced through directly to her heart.

She would do whatever it took to earn his trust back— and to be with him, even if only for a short while. He wasn't the marrying type, she knew. He wouldn't be interested in her for the long run. But whatever bit of love she could take, she would. She was no longer the frightened woman who would break in half if a man even threatened to walk out on her. If Andrea could break it off with a psycho like Rodney, she knew she could deal with anything.

The tour guide informed the group that the bus had finished its loop and was going back to the beginning. Andrea lunged out the door before the damn bus took her all the way back to the Empire State building. She had to find Mark, and fast.

Mark...please let me get to you before they do.

* * * * *

Mark sat on the living room floor with his niece Jaime, letting her comb his hair as he listened to his sister and mother chatter on excitedly about everything that had been going on since he had been gone.

"It's been way too long, Mark," his mother said with a smile. Her chestnut brown hair and sparkling green eyes left no doubt that she was Mark Cannon's mother. "You should come back more often."

"So...I like Andrea," Katherine said. "She's cute. And she's very interested in you."

Mark had to summon all of his acting abilities to answer nonchalantly. "Yeah, I like her too."

His sister smiled knowingly. "More than like, I should think."

Mark laughed. "You think?" Jaime squealed in delight as Mark stood, swooping her up in his arms.

The buzzer rang. His mom walked to the intercom by the front door. "Speak of the devil—that must be Andrea. She's here early." She spoke into the intercom as she pressed the button for the door to open. "Come on up, honey."

A few moments later there was a heavy knock on the door. Mark put Jaime down and bounded over to the door. It's funny—Andrea had been gone only a few hours and already he missed her.

But the face he saw in the peephole was not Andrea. Make that faces—there were two guys standing there. He didn't recognize them.

Mark looked back over his shoulder at his family. "It's

not Andrea. It's some guys. Are you expecting anyone?"

His brother-in-law shook his head. "Maybe they want your autograph or something."

Through the door he heard, "Hey, Mister Cannon, we gotta talk to you."

Katherine scowled and called, "There's no Mr. Cannon here, you've got the wrong building."

Silence on the other side of the door. Then, the voice said, "Tell him it's about Andrea."

Oh God.

Mark looked out the peephole again. What had happened to Andrea? He opened the door and stepped out into the hallway, instinctively closing the door behind him. He didn't like the looks of these guys and he didn't want them anywhere near his family. "Can I help you?" He kept his expression blank.

One of the large men took a step forward. "We got some bad news 'bout your girlfriend Andrea Landley." The man stood very still, his meaty hands unnaturally stiff at his sides.

Mark felt as if his stomach were being twisted in knots. "Where is she? Who are you?" Mark demanded.

"We're…independent contractors. You've heard of *The Hollywood Exposer*, right?" the meaty one said.

"Yeah, you've stolen my image and taken my picture and invaded my privacy and published out-and-out lies about me just to sell papers," Mark spat out.

"We didn't do nothin'. We're independent contractors. I ain't no writer, that's for sure," the man said with a gruff laugh. "This is about Andrea Landley."

Mark felt as if time had frozen. "What about her? What are you talking about?"

"She works for *The Exposer*."

Mark laughed wryly. "I know. She told me she worked there as a secretary and that she turned down an opportunity to sell me out."

"Told you she turned down that opportunity, huh," the

man said, a barely contained smirk on his broad, oily face.

Mark felt his breath catch in his throat. "Andrea works for me now. She's my personal assistant."

"She works for the tabloids. She's an undercover reporter."

"Liar," Mark said.

The two men stepped toward him. "The facts is the facts," one said. "I don't care if you believe us or not. Just take a look at this right here," he said, brandishing the latest copy of *The Hollywood Exposer.*

Mark grabbed the paper unceremoniously from the man and let his eyes drop to the page.

"Oh no. No, no, no, no." Candid shots of his family covered the front page. The headline read *Mark Cannon Abandons Family for Fame.* He scanned the article.

"He hasn't seen his family in almost a year," Mark Cannon's personal assistant and rumored lover Andrea Landley confesses.

Mark realized he was crumpling the paper in his grip but he didn't care. Lies jumped out at him as his vision blurred with anger. His work is more important than his family. His sister writes him letters begging him to come home but he ignores them.

And Andrea's name as the source, clear as day.

Mark couldn't believe it. "It's not her. It can't be her. This is fake."

"I'm sorry, buddy. This is her paystub. That's her address, right there," the man said, pointing to a crumpled white piece of paper.

Mark looked at the paystub in disbelief. Payment as an information source. An informer. A spy.

She had betrayed him. Mark thought back to every personal secret he had shared with her. He thought of the intimate moments they had experienced. Would it all be published on the front page of a sleazy tabloid?

He had let down his guard and been more honest with

her than with anyone he had ever known, and she had lied to him. She had lied about everything. She thought she would gain his trust by admitting to working at the tabloid but promising she'd never sell him out. But she had. And she sold him out before she even gave her little fake confession too.

Mark didn't want to believe it, but he realized that every moment they had together was probably recorded somewhere. Had she worn a wire?

Could Andrea really be so cold as to get him to bare his soul to her and then turn around and call her horrible boss at the tabloid and tell him every detail? A low moan escaped his throat at the thought of Andrea laughing at him behind his back.

The worst part of it was that Mark had been foolish enough to think that a woman might actually like him just for himself. The time that he shared with Andrea had been different than time he had spent with any other woman. She had genuinely seemed to care about the real Mark Cannon, not just the image. She didn't try to put him on a pedestal. She didn't seem to be after his money.

But it was all a lie. She seemed interested in the real Mark Cannon because she wanted to expose the real Mark Cannon. She wanted to lay him out, open and emotionally naked, in front of the whole world.

Mark handed the paper back to the men who stood in front of him. It was crumpled and sweaty from his hands.

The man took the paper from Mark. "Sorry to be the bearer of bad news, buddy."

Mark just shook his head, his teeth clenched together.

The other man whipped a camera out of his trench coat and flashed a quick picture of Mark's distressed face.

Mark closed his eyes and counted to ten slowly, trying to let his anger dissipate. When he opened them, the thugs were gone.

Mark went to the apartment door but it was locked. His hand trembled with anger as he knocked.

"It's me," he said, his voice thick with emotion. "Let me in."

CHAPTER TEN

Andrea sighed, watching the glittering gray city pass her by outside the taxi window. It was over. After Mark saw the tabloid article, the trust between them would be ruined forever along with her relationship with the only man she had ever loved.

"Just pull over right here," Andrea said to the driver. She handed him the fare and stepped out onto the sidewalk.

She stood in front of the tall gray building, looking at it with trepidation. "You know what? Maybe you should just keep that meter running and hang out here for a moment," she said, turning on her heels to face the cab. It was already gone.

Her pulse race as she walked up to the front door and rang the buzzer.

Mark answered, his deep baritone voice coming out of the rusty metal speaker near the buzzer. "Hello."

"Mark," Andrea said, speaking into the intercom. "It's Andrea."

"Stay there," he said. "I'll be right down."

She breathed a sigh of relief. He was talking to her. Maybe he hadn't seen the paper.

Andrea heard Mark's footsteps bounding down the tiny staircase. He opened the front door and stepped outside, letting it swing shut behind him. The black paint on the metal door was chipped.

"Mark, we need to talk," she said, her voice quavering slightly.

Mark shook his head, his muscular arms crossed in front of his broad chest. "There's nothing to say."

She felt tears well up in her eyes and blinked them back rapidly, trying to calm herself. She was a big girl. She could handle this.

"I need to tell you the truth—I'll tell you anything you want to know, Sir." She motioned toward the front door. "Can we at least step inside to the lobby?"

"No," Mark said. "We can't."

"I tried to call you, Sir."

"Honestly, I have no desire to speak to you. Ever again."

"Listen, please? There's no easy way to say this, Sir."

"No need to say anything at all. I already know everything. You lied to me. You betrayed me, Andrea."

"You're right, Mark, I did. I know that nothing that I say can fix this, but I need to at least try to explain."

"There's nothing to explain."

"Please, Mark," she said. "Let me just talk to you for a moment."

Mark raised his head and stared at her, his brow furrowed in anger.

Andrea took a deep breath. "Okay, here it is. When I confessed everything, I was telling you the truth. I did work as a secretary for *The Hollywood Exposer*."

Mark scowled.

"I didn't plan on getting any big scoops," she continued.

"So why'd you apply for the job, then?"

"I was sick of working as a secretary for Rodney and I wanted a new job," she admitted. "I was grateful to get the position."

"Nice way to show it," he growled. "Run my name into the mud."

"At the time, I didn't know you at all," she said. "All I knew was that my career at the tabloid was suddenly going places. My career was all I had."

A small muscle in Mark's jaw flexed as he listened to her, grinding his teeth. "How could you be so selfish? You only thought of yourself. You only thought of your career."

"It was the opportunity of a lifetime for me, Mark. I'm not the type of girl to get any breaks in life. I have to make them for myself."

"Because it's all about you, huh?" Mark said.

"I know it's hard to understand, but having this happen to me was like the equivalent of you getting your first big movie role. I had to take that chance, see? And then once I took that chance, I saw that I was on the wrong path. I couldn't work for Rodney and for you at the same time, because I realized the truth…"

"What truth?" Mark spat out.

"That my loyalties lay with you, and not with the tabloid like they were supposed to."

"What does he know about me? What did you tell him?" Mark asked.

"I never gave him any information at all about you. Not on purpose."

"You were paid as an informant, Andrea. I saw the check. So don't bother lying to me anymore."

"If there was a check, it's because when I went to Rodney's office to quit I mentioned—accidentally and in a very offhand way—that we were going to New York to see your sister because it had been a while."

"He knew about the letter she had sent me. The only one who knew about that was you."

"I-I may have slipped about that too. I'm sorry, I wasn't trying to sell you out. I swear."

"Why not?" he asked. "If you really thought this was your one big chance at tabloid journalism notoriety, then why did you blow it?"

"Once I had your trust, I just couldn't bring myself to break it," she said, her voice cracking. "I didn't want to be that person."

"You mean, you didn't want to be that person that made me lose my faith in the inherent goodness of people?" Mark asked, his voice harsh.

"Mark, I'm so sorry. Please forgive me. Punish me. Do whatever you need to do to make this right."

"It doesn't work that way. I don't think I can just forgive and forget this kind of thing, Andrea. And you don't want me to punish you when I'm angry—I don't have the control I need to not actually hurt you."

"I want you to hurt me. I want you to do whatever you need to do so I can be forgiven. Please, Sir."

"No." Mark took a deep breath in. "This isn't just a little mistake. This is huge. Really huge."

"I understand, Sir," she said, her breath catching in her throat, tears flowing over her face. "It's just—I'm not the same person I was when I worked for the tabloid. That wasn't me. This is me, right here. You changed me."

Mark stood silently, his broad shoulders hunched as he stared at the dirty New York sidewalk.

She wanted to reach out and just hold on to him, but she knew she couldn't.

"I can't even look at you right now," Mark said. "Go back to the airport. I'll have your suitcase shipped from the Ritz."

Andrea struggled to regain her composure. "I'm sorry I caused you so much pain. It was never my intention, Sir."

"I'll have a return ticket waiting for you at the ticket counter. Go back to L.A., go back to Rodney—" His voice caught on the word and he swallowed hard. "Do what you have to do."

* * * * *

Andrea nuzzled Peppers against her face and then wailed into her pillow. She had spent the entire cab ride back to the airport in New York as well as the entire flight back to Los Angeles thinking about what had happened. She had spent the past three days, in fact, going over and over the whole scenario.

It was no use. She had lost her one true love forever. Even the lash marks on her ass were fading, just as she was going to fade from Mark's memory.

There was a tentative knock on her bedroom door.

"Andrea?" Frannie's voice sounded muffled through the door.

Andrea sat up and blew her nose. "Come in, it's unlocked," she said.

"I'm worried about you, Andrea. You haven't left the house since you got home."

"There's no reason to leave. I don't have a job anymore. Not as a secretary, not as a reporter and not as Mark Cannon's assistant." A loud sob escaped her lips.

"Get up, Andrea. Why are you still in pajamas? You need to shower and get dressed and get yourself going."

Andrea shook her head. "What's the point?"

"If you really love him, you need to tell him," Frannie said, pushing her curls out of her eyes.

"I can't tell him that. Besides," she said, picking at a piece of lint on her flannel pajama bottoms, "Mark won't talk to me. He told me he doesn't even want to look at me."

Frannie sat on the edge of Andrea's bed, twirling a curl in concentration. "Oh my gosh. Today's the day you were supposed to be back from New York, right?"

"Right…"

"So you know what flight he's coming in on. Pick him up at the airport."

"I can't do that."

"Why not? Just do it. This may be your only chance to see him again."

"That's crazy…but it might be just crazy enough to actually work," Andrea said, releasing her grip on the cat.

Andrea stood and started for the door.

"Wait," Frannie said, jumping up.

Andrea whirled around and looked at her.

Frannie grinned. "Really, you need to shower first."

* * * * *

Mark moved as though he were in a daze. He hadn't slept well since—well, for the past three days. *Andrea.* He couldn't stop thinking about her.

Forget her. He needed to just move on. He could hear people in the airport whispering with excitement as he picked up his luggage from the baggage claim. He just wasn't in the mood for autograph seekers. He wasn't in the mood for anything. Mark pulled his baseball cap down as low as it would go and stepped outside into the bright Southern California weather.

Looking at the long line of taxicabs and shuttles outside baggage claim, Mark was glad that one of the crew members from the movie would be dropping off his car for him to drive home. The production company had offered a limo, of course, but Mark just wanted to be alone. No chauffeurs. No assistants or entourage. Just him and some private time. He needed to take a long, winding drive along the Pacific Coast Highway to clear his head.

Mark pulled out his cell phone and dialed. "I'm here."

* * * * *

Andrea pulled up outside baggage claim. Where was he? She looked around and checked her wristwatch in frustration. Her timing was off. He'd probably already gotten his luggage.

Suddenly she spotted him, his trademark thick, chestnut brown hair and famous face disguised by a white baseball cap and designer sunglasses.

"Mark," she yelled, hopping out of her car.

A whistle blew near her ear. A uniformed cop shouted to her over the honking of cars. "Ma'am. Move that car or it's going to get towed."

Andrea slid back into her car and opened the window. "Mark," she yelled again.

Either he didn't hear her or he thought she was some starstruck fan looking for a photo. Or maybe, she thought, he did hear her and he was ignoring her.

Andrea watched as Mark got into a bright red Porsche and pulled away from the curb.

She lowered her head on her steering wheel. He was gone. Again. Maybe it just wasn't meant to be.

"Move along." The cop blew his whistle, startling her.

"Okay, okay, I'm moving," she said, pulling away.

She navigated her way out to the freeway. It was a stupid idea anyway. There were other men out there. Other jobs. Here she was, behaving like a stalker, and for what? To tell a man who hated her that she loved him?

"You are so pathetic," she wailed, slamming her hand against the steering wheel. The worst part was, she knew there were no other men out there for her. Mark Cannon was the only one she wanted.

"Calm yourself." She didn't want to be without him, but she was strong enough now to be on her own if she had to. She wasn't going to settle.

Andrea's head jerked forward as the back of her car was knocked into on the freeway. *What the hell?*

Bam! The car behind her banged into her rear bumper again. She looked in her rear view mirror in confusion. What was going on?

Andrea saw the driver's pale face and gelled hair and a low moan escaped her. *Rodney.*

He pulled his car next to hers, driving aggressively. His passenger side window rolled down and Andrea looked out of her open window at him with contempt.

"What in the world are you doing, you jerk?" Andrea asked, even though there was no way he could hear her with the wind blowing.

Rodney kept his speed even with hers at about fifty

miles per hour. He yelled out the window to her. The words caught on the wind and all she heard was something about a cat and mouse.

Andrea could tell by his erratic driving that he'd had a few drinks.

"Rodney, pull over. You shouldn't be driving," she yelled, hoping her voice would carry on the freeway. The wind whipped in through her open window and swirled her hair around her face.

Rodney laughed and passed her.

Andrea watched in horror as Rodney sped off after a bright red Porsche.

He's after Mark.

* * * * *

Mark drove with the radio off, letting his thoughts flow over him. The trip to visit his family had been way too short, but he promised he'd visit them again once the movie was finished shooting. He didn't want to miss seeing his niece grow up.

He glanced at the passenger seat of the Porsche. It was empty. *Andrea should be sitting there.* Squirming in her seat from the crotch rope he had intended to put on her before the long drive home. Instead she was moving on with her life. Mark could have kicked himself for actually telling her to go back to Rodney.

He exited the main freeway and headed for the Pacific Coast Highway.

All he could think about during his whole trip in New York was Andrea Landley. He wanted to believe that she really did quit her job at the tabloid. Was it possible that she really didn't tell Rodney any of his secrets on purpose? That she was set up?

There was a time in his life when Mark was just looking for an excuse to keep himself distanced from a woman. He didn't want the commitment. He couldn't handle the distraction.

Mark looked out the windshield at the road ahead.

PCH was a beautiful but dangerous highway—narrow and twisty. He forced himself to slow down.

Every bone in his body ached with longing for Andrea. The three days that had passed since she'd left him standing on the sidewalk outside his sister's apartment had been the longest of his life.

But he shouldn't try to fool himself. Andrea didn't leave him standing there, he pushed her away. He had pushed her away out of fear. What if she tried to hurt him again? What if she was dishonest with him?

She had deceived him in the beginning, but ultimately she told the truth. She came clean. Andrea never meant to sell him out. She knew what she had done was hurtful and she had begged forgiveness.

But he hadn't given her the forgiveness. Mark knew that until he could forgive her transgression, he would always be haunted by fear.

Andrea was honest, he realized. She had become an honest woman. She had said it was because of him. Mark wondered if it was really possible—did his love change her?

Mark gripped the steering wheel tightly. Love?

He wasn't in love with Andrea...was he? Oh no. He was. He loved her.

He loved her tender smile. He loved her hungry kisses. He loved her refusal to give up no matter the circumstances. He loved the way she trusted him so completely in the bedroom, offering herself to him however he desired. He loved her long dark hair and he loved how she walked with him and his dog in the Hollywood Hills. He loved her willingness to help him, to be there for him.

Now he needed to be there for her.

Don't be crazy—she's gone. She was probably already back at the tabloid, already back with Rodney. Why should Mark think she would want to be with a self-absorbed actor like himself? She did have a life before she met him, and here he was expecting her to drop everything and run back to him just because he had decided he was ready.

Thinking about their last moments together, Mark knew he could never expect Andrea to love him. He had abandoned her in New York City. He made her fly all the way out there and then shoved her in a cab and sent her back across the country because he was angry with her.

As far as Andrea knew, he was the wham-bam-thank-you-ma'am type. What did she know about Mark's romantic affairs except that there was a different one splashed over the front pages of the tabloids every other week? She probably thought she was just another phone number in his little black book.

He needed to prove to Andrea that he was never going to leave her again.

He was ready to give up all the starlets and fashion models. He didn't want to be with anyone but Andrea.

He pulled his cell phone out and called her, keeping his eyes focused on the winding road in front of him.

It rang and rang, but only her voicemail picked up. "Andrea, it's Mark. Please call me."

He hung up and drove, praying that his phone would ring.

* * * * *

Andrea had to warn Mark that Rodney was following him. She reached for her cell phone.

It wasn't there.

Andrea felt around on the seat, glancing down quickly as she drove, looking for the phone. She always kept her cell phone in her purse, unless she was driving. Then she put it on vibrate and kept it on her lap so she could easily reach it while she was driving. She was way behind on the whole hands-free cell phone thing, and the threat of a ticket hadn't spurred her to get into it yet. She kept promising herself she'd get a Bluetooth headpiece but she never did.

Where was that stupid phone? It was on her lap when

she jumped out of the car at the airport. It was probably lying on the asphalt outside LAX in shiny little pieces.

Rodney's car up was up ahead. How was she going to warn Mark without her cell phone—before Rodney had the chance to catch up to him?

She had no choice. She would just have to join in this cat and mouse game.

* * * * *

Andrea couldn't see Mark's red Porsche anymore. The highway had twisted and turned so many times that he could easily be miles away. Rodney's car was in front of her, a small white dot always just around the bend.

She followed Rodney, figuring he had Mark's car in sight. She didn't know why Rodney was chasing after Mark. If only she had her cell phone, she could call Mark and warn him. She could call the police.

Even if she stopped and used a call box on the side of the road, Rodney would catch up with Mark before the police could. And she would come on the scene before the police would as well.

She didn't care if she got a speeding ticket. She just hoped she didn't crash.

Mark drove up the coastline, enjoying the view of the ocean. He loved the way the car hugged the lines of the road.

A flash of light glinted across his rear view mirror and Mark looked up in surprise. A white car was behind him, dangerously close to his tail. That moron—what did he want Mark to do, speed up? What was his hurry?

The car honked loudly and Mark cursed under his breath. There was no shoulder on this part of the highway. There was no way for him to pull over safely to let the impatient driver pass.

To Mark's surprise, the white car veered to the side, crossing the double yellow line. Mark expected him to pass him in a flurry of honking horns, but the car pulled up next to him.

Mark looked over at him in amazement and was immediately blinded by a flash of light. The man was taking pictures, blinding him with his camera.

"Paparazzi!" Mark yelled it like it was a curse word.

The man called out something Mark couldn't hear and kept snapping photos at a breakneck speed.

"Get out of here, you're going to kill us both," Mark yelled out the window. The guy didn't look like he heard him, but then he shouted something back as he lowered the camera and grinned at Mark.

Oh great. It was Rodney. Again.

"Rodney—get out of here. There's no room for passing on this section of the highway—don't be insane," Mark yelled, knowing that his voice wouldn't carry over the freeway. As much as he hated the creep, he didn't want him to get hit by an oncoming car and die.

Rodney either was ignoring him or couldn't hear him, flashing his camera to prove a point. He wasn't even looking at the twisting road ahead of them.

Mark saw a huge truck coming around the bend. "*Truck!*" he yelled.

Rodney wasn't looking—he was clicking his camera in Mark's direction.

"Truck!" Mark yelled louder, pointing at the road in front of Rodney's car.

Rodney saw the huge truck barreling toward him and let out a high-pitched scream. Mark watched in horror as Rodney dropped the camera and grabbed hold of the steering wheel in a panic.

Mark could see Rodney twist the wheel, the little white car's wheels screeching in protest, making black skid marks on the highway. Rodney cut his car sharply in front of Mark's, missing the truck by mere inches.

Mark was grateful for the Porsche's ability to stop on a dime as he narrowly avoided hitting the back of Rodney's car. The truck had simply stopped in the middle of the road and the trucker was climbing out, anger written all over his face as he yelled a stream of curses at Rodney. Rodney actually pulled over as much as the narrow highway would allow and started screaming back at him like the drunken idiot he was.

Mark honked at the two men, unable to get past the vehicles. Sighing, Mark called 9-1-1. Someone needed to put Rodney's ass in jail ASAP.

Another car horn blared behind him. Annoyed, Mark gestured to indicate that he couldn't move past. The car horn beeped again, two short beeps this time. Mark turned around in his bucket seat and grinned. *Andrea.*

* * * * *

Andrea left the key in the ignition and stepped out of her car, walking at first and then running toward Mark. Mark stepped out of his car and took a tentative step toward her before standing still. Andrea could hear Rodney and the trucker still going at it in the middle of the road but all she cared about right now was Mark.

"I'm so glad you're okay," she said.

"What are you doing here?" he asked. She couldn't tell if he was angry or pleased because his voice was so level, so calm—when all of her nerves felt jangled and undone.

"I-I tried to pick you up at the airport so I could properly apologize to you, and then I followed you when I saw that Rodney was following you, so…here I am. Sir."

Mark shook his head and Andrea swallowed hard in disappointment. Why was he shaking his head? Because she had followed him, or because she was still trying to apologize, or because he thought she was pathetic?

The police finally arrived and pulled to a stop behind Andrea's car, their lights flashing as the young cop got out and surveyed the scene.

"I'm the one that called," Mark said to the officer, avoiding Andrea's eyes, "because that man is drunk driving and nearly got us all killed."

The officer nodded and approached Rodney and the trucker with caution as the two men continued to scream at each other.

Andrea ignored the commotion and focused on Mark. It might be the last time she ever saw him again. "Mark, please, I don't know what to say to make this right."

Andrea felt tears run down her face as she looked at Mark just standing there on the side of the highway, their cars abandoned in the road.

Mark took two long strides toward her and wrapped her in his arms, kissing her forehead. "Say you forgive me," he said, kissing her again, this time on her trembling lips.

"Forgive you? But, Sir, I'm the one—"

"No, I'm the one who screwed everything up. Trust me on this. You're the best thing that's ever happened to me. Those three days we were apart were the worst three days of my life."

"I know," Andrea said. "I spent them hiding under the covers, sobbing."

"I never want to be apart from you like that again. I-I love you, Andrea."

"I love you too, Sir." Warmth rushed through her and she just knew, instinctively, that it was love she was feeling in her bones. "I'm yours."

Mark picked her up then, cradling her in his arms, crushing her against his muscular torso. "I'm not letting you go ever again. I'm kidnapping you," he said, walking over to his Porsche with her in his arms.

"What about my car?" she protested, laughing even as she thrilled at his words. "I can't just leave it here."

"I'll have someone take care of it," Mark said. The cop had arrested Rodney and was impounding Rodney's car, and the trucker had pulled to the side of the road. The road was clear enough for them to get by.

Mark carefully placed Andrea into the passenger seat and buckled her in with the seatbelt. Reaching into his glove compartment, he grabbed a roll of duct tape and showed it to Andrea with a grin.

Andrea gasped. What was he going to do with that? She looked out the window, wondering what that cop was going to think of all this, but he was already gone. They were alone on the highway...

"Give me your hands," Mark ordered.

Andrea complied, offering her hands to him with a small smile on her face.

"You don't have to tie me up, I swear I won't escape, Sir," she said, excited that he would bind her anyway.

Mark wrapped the duct tape around her wrists and then crossed her ankles and taped them together as well. Between the tape and the seat belt, she really couldn't escape even if she wanted to.

Of course, she was exactly where she wanted to be.

"I can't have you screaming for help, so I'm going to tape your mouth," he said as he pressed a piece of tape over her lips. "You're mine now."

Andrea felt her pussy get wet at his words and she tried to lick her lips before being abruptly reminded of the tape over her mouth. Mark got into the driver's seat and shut the door, locking them in. He reached over her to get back into the glove box and she could smell the excitement on him, a heady, musky scent that turned her on.

"I was planning on having you ride home with a crotch rope, so I picked this up in New York," he said, pulling out a handful of nylon rope. "And to think, just when I was getting all depressed about how I'd never get to see you squirm again, here you are. My captive."

Mark opened her belt and the top buttons of her jeans and made a knot in the length of rope. He slid the rope between her legs, inside her underwear, so that the knot pressed directly on her clit. Andrea gasped but the sound was muffled by the tape.

"Look how easy you made this for me." Mark smiled as he pulled up her jeans and wrapped the ends of the rope around her belt, tying them tightly. The pressure on her clit was immediate and insistent, tugging at her delicate nub as she wriggled in her bonds.

"We've got a long drive home, so you just enjoy that sensation for a while." Mark grinned at her and put the car in gear.

It was a bumpy ride.

EPILOGUE
ONE YEAR LATER

"The limo will be here soon, Sir," Andrea said.

"Let them wait," Mark said. "This is more important."

Andrea eyed him nervously as he pulled some sort of contraption out from behind his back. "Sir?"

"It's a chastity belt—I had it specially made just for you. It has a pussy plug, an anal plug, and a lock that only I will have the key for." Mark looked at her with a twinkle in his eye. "I know the butt plug looks big—I want to stretch you out a bit."

"Right now, Sir? Right before your movie premiere?"

"Yup. You'll be wearing this under your dress all evening. It should make sitting through the boring bits of the movie a little more exciting for you—and for me."

Andrea lifted her billowy dress and gasped as she felt the lubricated plugs slide into place. Even with all the anal sex they'd been having since she had moved into his mansion, the plug he got for her ass stretched her uncomfortably. "Sir, I can't wear this…please!"

Mark grinned. "You're wearing it. No more protests."

"But, Sir—" she started to say. She shut her mouth quickly when she saw him pull out a small vibrating bullet.

"I told you no more protests, Andrea. Now you're having this little devil tucked in there too until the battery dies on it." He slid it directly onto her clit and then locked the chastity belt into place.

Andrea's jaw dropped as she took a step forward, letting the dress drop around her. Every step was pure orgasmic heaven—or hell, depending on how long it was going to last. Which, knowing Mark as well as she did, was going to be for hours.

"Let's go, honey," he said, taking her hand.

It took them an hour in traffic before they arrived at the theater, during which time Andrea was sure she had reached her orgasm limit. Fortunately the battery on the vibrating bullet wore out within the hour, and now she was just left with the hard nub rubbing insistently against her clit as she squirmed in her seat, trying to find a comfortable spot and only succeeding in nudging the plugs deep inside her.

Andrea looked out the limousine window nervously. "Mark, there are a lot of people out there."

Mark laughed. "That's what a movie premiere is all about. Just remember to smile for the cameras. You look gorgeous, sweetheart."

Andrea smiled. "You look pretty good yourself," she said with a wink.

It was true. She couldn't believe that after all the hard work, they were finally going to be able to walk down the red carpet at the premiere.

"Are you nervous about the paparazzi?" she asked.

"No, not really. This is where they're supposed to be, at events like this. It's expected. It's part of my job. I just don't like it when they stalk me when I'm off the clock, so to speak."

"After your experiences, I wouldn't blame you if you were a little wary."

"Think of what Frannie would say if we skipped this," Mark said with a laugh.

"That's true, Sir," Andrea said. "I think she's even more excited about it than we are. She's invited Steve over to watch the red carpet show."

"Isn't Steve that gaffer with the glasses? I knew Frannie had something going on with him. Good for her," he said.

"Mark, I'm nervous. There're a lot of people out there."

"Don't worry about it," he said, nuzzling his face against her cheek. "Are you ready?"

"Ready when you are, Sir."

Mark nudged Andrea gently. "Okay, let's do this," he said, his brown hair looking perfectly tousled.

The limo door was opened and a man in a tuxedo helped her to step onto the red carpet gracefully. Mark stepped out after her and all of the paparazzi turned in unison and flashed their cameras at the star of the movie.

Mark held out his arm for Andrea and she took a deep breath and stepped in place next to him, grateful that the material of her gown concealed the hard edge of her chastity belt.

Andrea could hear reporters talking loudly in excited tones into their microphones, their coiffed hair not even swaying in the gentle Southern California breeze.

"And here comes the star of the movie, Mark Cannon." A heavily Botoxed television personality clapped her hands exuberantly and waved him over to her cameraman, who was videotaping her for her celebrity news show.

Mark grinned at Andrea and they made their way up the red carpet to her.

"Mark Cannon—they say this movie is going to be huge. How's it feel?" the reporter asked with a wink.

"Feels great," he said, his deep baritone reverberating into her microphone.

"And who's the lovely lady? What are you wearing?"

Andrea swallowed hard. "I'm Andrea Landley, and I'm wearing a dress by Giorgio Armani," she said.

"She's a reporter for *The L.A. Times*," Mark chimed in.

Andrea smiled. She had Frannie to thank for her new job. Frannie had secretly submitted some of her work to the editors at *The Times*, and with the subsequent publicity her name got from being attached to Mark Cannon, she was offered a position on a paper she could only have dreamed of writing for back when she was working at *The Hollywood Exposer*.

"Andrea Landley," the hostess said, laughing throatily. "Of course—the woman whose charms have kept you from your usual merry-go-round of dates."

Mark grinned and put a protective arm around Andrea. "This is the only woman I need," Mark said.

Andrea felt a blush spread over her lightly made-up face.

"Actually, I have an announcement to make," Mark said, his voice wafting above the low murmur of the crowd. All of the cameramen focused on him.

Andrea looked at Mark in shock. "You do?"

Mark slowly dropped to one knee, his intense green eyes never leaving her face.

"Oh my goodness, Mark…what are you doing?" Her breath caught in her throat, her heart going a mile a minute.

"I love you, Andrea," he said, staring up into her eyes. "I want to spend the rest of my life with you. I want to have children with you. I want to wake up next to your beautiful face every morning for the rest of my life."

A tear of joy ran down Andrea's cheek. She had cried so many tears over this man. But this was one teardrop she would cherish.

Mark reached into the inner pocket of his suit and pulled out a blue ring box. "Andrea Landley, will you marry me?"

Andrea gasped as he opened the box. Inside was a beautiful, huge princess cut diamond set in a simple platinum band.

"Yes. Yes, of course I'll marry you."

Mark stood, taking her left hand. Cameras flashed all around them. He slipped the diamond onto her ring finger.

There, on the center of the red carpet, with the whole world to witness the moment, Mark pulled her close and kissed her.

The End

ABOUT SHOSHANNA EVERS

Critically-acclaimed author Shoshanna Evers has written dozens of sexy stories including Amazon Erotica Bestsellers *Overheated*, and *Enslaved, Book 1 in the Enslaved Trilogy*, as well as the post-apocalyptic dystopian *Pulse Trilogy* from Simon & Schuster Pocket Star. Her work has been featured in *Best Bondage Erotica 2012* and *Best Bondage Erotica 2013*, the Penguin/Berkley Heat anthology *Agony/Ecstasy*, and numerous erotic BDSM novellas including *Chastity Belt* and *Punishing the Art Thief* from Ellora's Cave Publishing.

The non-fiction anthology Shoshanna Evers edited and contributed to, *How To Write Hot Sex: Tips from Multi-Published Erotic Romance Authors*, is a #1 Bestseller in the Authorship, Erotica Writing Reference, and Romance Writing categories on Amazon.

Reviewers have called Shoshanna's writing "fast paced, intense, and sexual…every naughty fantasy come to life for the reader" with stories where "the plot is fresh and the pacing excellent, the emotions…real and poignant."

Shoshanna used to work as a syndicated advice columnist and a registered nurse, but now she's a full-time smut writer and a home-schooling mom. She lives with her family and two big dogs in Northern Idaho.

Shoshanna Evers wants you to stay in touch!
Like erotic romance? Sign up for Shoshanna Evers's mailing list to be notified when a new book releases (right side of the page at **ShoshannaEvers.com/blog**)

Visit **ShoshannaEvers.com** for monthly giveaways and red-hot excerpts!
Let's be BFF's!
Connect on Twitter @ShoshannaEvers
and on Facebook.com/shoshanna.evers